Stephen King

WHO
WROTE
THAT?

Stephen King

Michael Gray Baughan

Foreword by
Kyle Zimmer

CHELSEA HOUSE
P U B L I S H E R S
An imprint of Infobase Publishing

Stephen King

Chelsea House
An imprint of Infobase Publishing
132 West 31st Street
New York NY 10001

Library of Congress Cataloging-in-Publication Data
Baughan, Michael Gray, 1973-
 Stephen King / Michael Gray Baughan.
 p. cm. — (Who wrote that?)
 Includes bibliographical references and index.
 ISBN 978-0-7910-9852-3 (hardcover)
 1. King, Stephen—Juvenile literature. 2. Novelists, American—20th century—
Biography—Juvenile literature. 3. Horror tales—Authorship—Juvenile literature. I.
Title. II. Series.
 PS3561.I483Z52 2009
 813'.54—dc22
 [B]   2008035031

Chelsea House books are available at special discounts when purchased in bulk quantities for business, associations, institutions, or sales promotions. Please call our Special Sales Department in New York at (212) 967-8800 or (800) 322-8755.

You can find Chelsea House on the World Wide Web at http://www.chelseahouse.com

Text design by Keith Trego and Erika Arroyo
Cover design by Alicia Post

Printed in the United States of America

Bang EJB 10 9 8 7 6 5 4 3 2 1

This book is printed on acid-free paper.

Table of Contents

FOREWORD BY
KYLE ZIMMER
PRESIDENT, FIRST BOOK

HUMANITY IS POWERED by stories. From our earliest days as thinking beings, we employed every available tool to tell each other stories. We danced, drew pictures on the walls of our caves, spoke, and sang. All of this extraordinary effort was designed to entertain, recount the news of the day, explain natural occurrences—and then gradually to build religious and cultural traditions and establish the common bonds and continuity that eventually formed civilizations. Stories are the most powerful force in the universe; they are the primary element that has distinguished our evolutionary path.

Our love of the story has not diminished with time. Enormous segments of societies are devoted to the art of storytelling. Book sales in the United States alone topped $24 billion in 2006; movie studios spend fortunes to create and promote stories; and the news industry is more pervasive in its presence than ever before.

There is no mystery to our fascination. Great stories are magic. They can introduce us to new cultures, or remind us of the nobility and failures of our own, inspire us to greatness or scare us to death; but above all, stories provide human insight on a level that is unavailable through any other source. In fact, stories connect each of us to the rest of humanity not just in our own time, but also throughout history.

This special magic of books is the greatest treasure that we can hand down from generation to generation. In fact, that spark in a child that comes from books became the motivation for the creation of my organization, First Book, a national literacy program with a simple mission: to provide new books to the most disadvantaged children. At present, First Book has been at work in hundreds of communities for over a decade. Every year children in need receive millions of books through our organization and millions more are provided through dedicated literacy institutions across the United States and around the world. In addition, groups of people dedicate themselves tirelessly to working with children to share reading and stories in every imaginable setting from schools to the streets. Of course, this Herculean effort serves many important goals. Literacy translates to productivity and employability in life and many other valid and even essential elements. But at the heart of this movement are people who love stories, love to read, and want desperately to ensure that no one misses the wonderful possibilities that reading provides.

When thinking about the importance of books, there is an overwhelming urge to cite the literary devotion of great minds. Some have written of the magnitude of the importance of literature. Amy Lowell, an American poet, captured the concept when she said, "Books are more than books. They are the life, the very heart and core of ages past, the reason why men lived and worked and died, the essence and quintessence of their lives." Others have spoken of their personal obsession with books, as in Thomas Jefferson's simple statement: "I live for books." But more compelling, perhaps, is the almost instinctive excitement in children for books and stories.

Throughout my years at First Book, I have heard truly extraordinary stories about the power of books in the lives of children. In one case, a homeless child, who had been bounced from one location to another, later resurfaced—and the only possession that he had fought to keep was the book he was given as part of a First Book distribution months earlier. More recently, I met a child who, upon receiving the book he wanted, flashed a big smile and said, "This is my big chance!" These snapshots reveal the true power of books and stories to give hope and change lives.

As these children grow up and continue to develop their love of reading, they will owe a profound debt to those volunteers who reached out to them—a debt that they may repay by reaching out to spark the next generation of readers. But there is a greater debt owed by all of us—a debt to the storytellers, the authors, who have bound us together, inspired our leaders, fueled our civilizations, and helped us put our children to sleep with their heads full of images and ideas.

WHO WROTE THAT? is a series of books dedicated to introducing us to a few of these incredible individuals. While we have almost always honored stories, we have not uniformly honored storytellers. In fact, some of the most important authors have toiled in complete obscurity throughout their lives or have been openly persecuted for the uncomfortable truths that they have laid before us. When confronted with the magnitude of their written work or perhaps the daily grind of our own, we can forget that writers are people. They struggle through the same daily indignities and dental appointments, and they experience the intense joy and bottomless despair that many of us do. Yet somehow they rise above it all to deliver a powerful thread that connects us all. It is a rare honor to have the opportunity that these books provide to share the lives of these extraordinary people. Enjoy.

Stephen King at the New York premiere of The Green Mile *on December 8, 1999. Earlier that year, on June 19, he was struck by a van and nearly killed while out on his daily stroll.*

1

Opening Doors

STEPHEN KING SET out for his daily stroll on the afternoon of June 19, 1999, with no idea of what was in store for
him. Like any of the hundreds of characters who populate
his fictional universe, he was just a regular guy, going about
his regular day, about to collide headlong with extraordinary
circumstances.

Bryan Smith had a long list of moving violations on his
record, but he was not drunk and it was broad daylight. On any
other day, he might have driven his Dodge van right on by, perhaps not even noticing the lanky fellow on the side of Route 5.
But on that day, Stephen King just happened to ascend an
uphill section of road that blocked his view of oncoming traffic

at the precise moment Smith swerved onto the shoulder and came barreling over the hill with his head turned away from the road in front of him. Smith would later explain that he was trying to keep one of his dogs from nosing its way into a cooler filled with meat.[1]

The collision sent King flying 14 feet in the air, over the van and into a ditch. Fortunately, King was lucky enough to miss both the harder section of the van's grill and some large rocks at the roadside that would almost certainly have killed him. Nevertheless, his body was broken in enough places to rival Humpty Dumpty. For the next several hours, King clung to life, slipping in and out of consciousness as help arrived and rushed him to the closest hospital. When one of his lungs collapsed, an emergency medical technician was forced to puncture his chest and insert a breathing tube. The man told his famous patient that it would not hurt very much. This little white lie, used by doctors and nurses the world over, held special meaning for King. The first time he heard it, he was just six years old and on the cusp of becoming a writer.

ON THE MOVE

The doctor promised it wouldn't hurt, but one look at the needle told little Stephen King otherwise. Not to mention *where* he was planning on sticking it. As a boy, King had suffered through a string of common childhood illnesses that had culminated in an ear infection severe enough to require the attention of a specialist. The only solution was to have it drained, and that meant sticking a long needle straight through his eardrum.

King never forgot the pain of that procedure. It did not help that not only was he forced to endure it several more times before the infection went away, but what really got to him were the doctor's repeated promises that "*this* time it wouldn't hurt."[2]

Who to trust must have been a difficult question for Stephen as a boy. His early years were a blur of constant moves and uncertainty, set off by one major abandonment: Born in Portland, Maine, on September 21, 1947, Stephen Edwin King only had a couple of years to know his father before the man disappeared from his life forever. Donald King was a traveling salesman for Electrolux, an early appliance company that specialized in vacuum cleaners. One day, he left their home in Durham for a pack of cigarettes and simply never came back.

Stephen's mother, Nellie Ruth Pillsbury King, was a homemaker with no special skills beyond a knack for survival. Years earlier, she had been told by her doctor that she was unable to have children, so in 1945 she and her husband adopted a boy and named him David. Two years later, to the Kings' great surprise, little Stevie was born. Two years after that, Donald King deserted the family. Nellie was faced with the task of raising two boys with no immediate source of income.

For the next several years, Nellie shuttled David and Stephen from one relative to the next, living with the boys in five different states before returning to Durham in 1958. During that time, she held a number of odd jobs to make ends meet and saw little of her children. Her time and energy were taxed even more back in Maine, where she took on the responsibility of caring for her aging parents. For the latter half of his childhood, Stephen lived in his grandparents' house, in a semirural part of Durham known as Methodist Corners. Nearby was a one-room schoolhouse, where he attended fifth and sixth grades.

DEATH LESSONS

When Stephen was four and playing outside unsupervised, one of his playmates was hit and killed by a train. Afterward, Stephen wandered home by himself in a daze, unable to tell his mother what had happened. To this day, King says that he has no conscious memory of the incident. His next brush with death came a few years later, when he discovered that his grandmother had died in her sleep. This time, the experience stuck with him and would eventually influence a short story called "Gramma."

Later in life, interviewers would often ask King if these events could explain why he wrote scary stories, as if his fertile imagination and his desire to explore frightening subjects were simply the side effects of post-traumatic stress disorder. King discounts this notion. "I believe this is a totally specious idea—such shoot-from-the-hip psychological judgments are little more than jumped-up astrology."[3] Elsewhere, though, he does suggest an *apotropaic,* or superstitious, component to his writing. "Another reason that I've always written horror is because it's a kind of psychological protection. It's like drawing a magic circle around myself and my family."[4]

FIRST SALE

Due to illness, Stephen missed enough of the first grade that he was forced to repeat it the following year. Meanwhile, his older brother, David, excelled in his studies and was able to skip third grade entirely. While at home recovering, Stephen gorged himself on comic books and adventure tales by Jack London and other authors, and, before long, he was writing stories of his own. At first, he simply copied the plots from his comic books. When he showed these "stories" to Nellie, Stephen found he enjoyed the motherly pride she displayed. The feeling was soon replaced with embarrassment, however, when he owned up to his plagiarism. His mother suggested he could do much better writing his own stories. The idea lit a spark in young Stephen. He longed to recapture that warm glow of accomplishment, but he was also enchanted by the chance to create and explore literally *anything* his mind could imagine. "I remember an immense feeling of possibility," he recalls in his memoir, "as if I had been ushered into a vast building filled with closed doors and had been given leave to open any I liked. There were more doors than one person could ever open in a lifetime."[5]

Some writers toil away for many years before they see a penny for their efforts, and some writers never make any money at all. To them, writing often becomes an abstract pursuit, dependent on the whims of inspiration, instead of a regular job that requires daily labor like any other. It was Stephen King's good fortune to have a mother who was wise and practical enough to teach him the difference. When her son came back to her with an original story of his own (about a heroic team of crusading animals), she not only told him "it was good enough to be in a book," she proceeded to pay him a quarter for each of the next four installments. "That was the first buck I made in the business," King proudly remembers.[6] The lesson was not lost on her son, although the concept of copyright infringement took a little longer to sink in. A few years later, after seeing the 1961 film version of Edgar Allan

Poe's story, "The Pit and Pendulum," Stephen hit upon the idea of "novelizing" the movie for sale to his classmates. He sold dozens of this eight-page adaptation and made nearly $10 before the school principal stepped in and put a halt to his cottage industry. Ironically, it was not the plagiarism that offended Miss Hisler, nor was she bothered by his use of the school as a marketplace. Rather, she objected to the content of the story and chastised him for wasting his talent on "junk."[7] King would spend the rest of his career fighting against the same kind of highbrow literary criticism.

DAVE'S RAG

King also credits his older brother, David, with being a major influence on him in his youth. Like many hyper-intelligent kids, David King was prone to wild flights of fancy that were high on imagination and low on common sense. One such early escapade resulted in the Kings' eviction from their apartment in Wisconsin after a neighbor found the six-year-old boy alone on the roof. Later, when inspired to outdo his fellow inventors in a grade-school science fair, Dave tried to "upgrade" a simple dry cell battery. He wrapped some bare electrical cord around it and asked his little brother to plug it in. Luckily, the pair of inventors survived. The power transformer on the street outside did not.

It was in this same spirit of foolhardy enterprise that David King launched his own amateur newspaper. *Dave's Rag* was aptly named. Initially printed on a primitive form of press known as a hectograph (sometimes called a jellygraph), the biweekly publication cost five cents a copy and featured local news, weather, jokes, and, of course, advertisements for stories by his little brother Stevie. Like

Stephen's *Pit and the Pendulum* experiment, these "stories" were initially abridged versions of classic books, such as *The Adventures of Tom Sawyer* and *Kidnapped*. Eventually, David got his hands on a used mimeograph machine and started to crank out dozens of copies of *Dave's Rag* for sale to friends and neighbors. He also shot and developed his own photographs in a homemade dark room in the basement. In the meantime, Stephen used the mimeograph to continue printing and selling his novel adaptations. Although barely into their teens, the King boys were proving to be a regular publishing industry.

VILLAGE VOMIT

With fewer than 1,000 residents, Durham could not support a high school, so Stephen was bussed to nearby Lisbon Falls. Because his town could not afford a real bus, King and his classmates rode to school in a converted funeral hearse instead.[8]

There was no movie theater in Durham either, so until he could drive, Stephen hitchhiked to nearby Lewiston just about every weekend. He was enthralled by all entertainment media, from early horror comics to radio cliffhangers and television shows, but nothing compared to the thrill he got from watching the big screen. Very early on, Stephen gravitated away from the "wholesome" films shown at the first-run theater and toward the "B" movies playing in a second-run joint across town. He recalled, "Horror movies, science fiction movies, movies about teenage gangs on the prowl, movies about losers on motorcycles—this was the stuff that turned my dials up to ten."[9]

Stephen's overactive imagination continued to get him into hot water at school. Tired of the boring material he slogged through as the editor of his high-school newspaper, he decided to write and publish a one-time parody newspaper he called *The Village Vomit*. He filled it with juvenile humor and made-up stories about his teachers that poked fun at their names and physical features. Accounts differ as to whether this stunt earned Stephen a suspension or just a string of detentions, but one thing is certain—his teachers were not happy. They came up with a plan to keep him busy with "real work," so he wouldn't have time to stir up any more trouble. As a result, Stephen was essentially forced into covering local sports for the Lisbon *Weekly Enterprise*. Beyond a burgeoning obsession with the Boston Red Sox, Stephen was not that much of a sports fan and quickly chafed at the confines of journalistic writing. He does, however, credit his boss at the *Enterprise* with teaching him more about editing and revising than all of his English teachers combined.

TURNING POINTS

When Stephen King was 12 or 13, the ghost of his father materialized in the form of an old box he found in the attic above his aunt and uncle's garage. In the box was a small hoard of Donald King's books that suggested little Stevie might have inherited his love of science fiction and horror from his absent father. Among the items were a few pulp novels, an anthology of *Weird Tales* comics, and—most influential of all—a collection of tales by H.P. Lovecraft. This last book gave Stephen what he has called his "first taste of a world that went deeper than the B-pictures which played at the movies on Saturday afternoon."[10] While often criticized for his melodramatic prose, Lovecraft is nevertheless considered a direct literary descendant of Edgar Allen Poe in the bloodline of America's greatest horror writers.

Another big step was taken when Stephen got his first typewriter. "It took me to the place where the physical act of writing wasn't uncomfortable any longer," he said in a 1984 interview with Douglas Winter. "I also finally had the means to prepare manuscripts that people might actually look at for publication."[11]

Shortly afterward, Stephen submitted his first original short story to a science fiction magazine called *Spacemen*. The story was not accepted. Undaunted, Stephen continued to send new stories to various publications until a nail on his bedroom wall held a thick sheaf of rejection slips. The vast majority of these rejections were form letters, with little to no constructive criticism, but at 16 he finally received a personal response from an editor at *Fantasy and Science Fiction* that included a few words of praise. It wasn't as good as an acceptance letter, but that small bit

Did you know...

Stephen King wrote his first novel when he was only 16. Entitled *The Aftermath*, it told the story of a nuclear holocaust survivor who sets out to destroy a super computer intent on wiping out the rest of humanity. Though never published, the novel was "remarkably mature" according to one early biographer.[14] Anyone wishing to read it can find the original manuscript in the special collections at the University of Maine at Orono, King's alma mater.

of encouragement meant the world to Stephen and stoked his fire anew.

By his own admission, King had yet to find his voice: "These stories had the trappings of science fiction—they were set in outer space—but they were really horror stories."[12] Deep down, he knew that to carve out an individual style for himself, he had to find a way to tap into his own personal experience.

If H.P. Lovecraft taught Stephen that writing horror could be a serious business, Richard Matheson showed him how to make it hit home. After he had read Matheson's novel *I Am Legend*, which has been adapted three times as a film, including a recent version starring Will Smith, Stephen came to realize "that horror didn't have to happen in a haunted castle; it could happen in the suburbs, on your street, maybe right next door."[13]

"TEEN-AGE GRAVEROBBER"

While waiting for his big break, Stephen continued to self-publish collections of his stories on his brother's mimeograph machine. He also enlisted a childhood friend named Chris Chesley as a collaborator. Their vanity press went by a number of names (Triad Publishing, Gaslight Books) and a couple of their amateur publications likely still exist today, in the vaults of King collectors, no doubt. The titles of these stories—"The Thing at the Bottom of the Well," "The Cursed Expedition"—reveal a young writer still under the influence of B-grade entertainment, but by all accounts Stephen took his craft very seriously.

King was finally rewarded for all his effort in 1965 when his story "I Was a Teen-Age Graverobber" appeared in a comic book fanzine called *Comics Review*. It was not the most auspicious print debut, but at least it hadn't come out of his basement.

Above, the August 12, 1966 issue of Time, *depicting mass murderer Charles Whitman, whose shooting rampage at the University of Texas shocked the nation and inspired a very young Stephen King to write an early novel about a high school student who murders several teachers and takes classmates hostage.*

2

Writing
His Head Off

STEPHEN KING GRADUATED from Lisbon Falls High School in 1966. Instead of enjoying a last carefree summer before college, he spent the summer working in a dingy old textile mill to help his mother make ends meet. When fellow workers told him about the monstrous rats that lived in the basement, King stashed that little spine-tingling tidbit into his Pandora's box of story ideas.

In the meantime, Stephen began to write another novel called *Getting It On,* about a high school student who shoots several of his teachers and takes his classmates hostage. Like most teenagers, King harbored his fair share of resentment and alienation. "Inside I felt different and unhappy a lot of times," he once confided. "I felt violent a lot of times. But I kept that part to myself."[1] Unlike his protagonist, King had a constructive outlet for his angst. "Maybe I couldn't put one past the centerfielder . . . but I could write."[2] A more specific inspiration for his novel came from the campus shootings at the University of Texas in August 1966. Charles Whitman climbed the UT tower and picked off some of his classmates with a sniper rifle. Given the number of similar tragedies that have happened since, it may be difficult for young people to understand just how much this shocked the nation at the time. King would explore this topic more explicitly in a short story entitled "Cain Rose Up," originally published in *Ubris* in the spring of 1968 and later collected in his 1985 anthology, *Skeleton Crew*.

KING'S GARBAGE TRUCK

Unable to afford the more expensive, out-of-state colleges, King enrolled at the University of Maine, in a town near Bangor called Orono. He majored in English and did fairly well as a student by keeping distractions to a minimum. As his wife, Tabitha, later recalled, "All he cared about was getting everything he could out of school and writing his head off."[3]

And write he did. Freshman year, he finished a short but harrowing novel called *The Long Walk*, about teenage contestants in a government-sponsored death march. Though the manuscript impressed several of his professors, it failed to garner any notice in a first-novel competition and would not be published for 13 years.

As a sophomore, King secured his first respectable credit when *Startling Mystery Stories* published "The Glass Floor" in their fall edition. He earned only $35 for his story, but at least he was now getting paid. That same year, he began work on another novel called *Sword in the Darkness*, King's attempt to capture the drama and violence of race relations during the civil rights era. Though he later disowned the manuscript, King felt strongly enough about it at the time to submit an unfinished draft to a New York publisher. In fact, he continued to revise and submit it until it was rejected by a dozen publishers. During that time, he also finished *Getting It On* and received some much-needed encouragement by publishing several more short stories.

When he wasn't writing fiction, King gained a little notoriety as the author of a weekly column called "King's Garbage Truck" in the college newspaper, in which he gave his opinion on everything from the latest music records and movies to current events.

Practical as ever, Nellie King convinced her son to develop a back up plan in case his writing career didn't take off quite as quickly as he hoped. Toward that end, King charted a course of study that would earn him a high school teaching credential upon graduation, in addition to a bachelor's degree in English. He also enrolled in several creative writing and poetry courses, but like many natural born storytellers, he found the academic writing environment stifling and unproductive.

MEETING TABITHA

Not everything about King's writing classes failed to stimulate him. When bored with the coursework, he could always gaze at the pretty legs of a classmate named Tabitha Spruce. The two had met the previous summer when they both worked at the college library to help offset the cost of tuition. Lukewarm first impressions changed into a mutual attraction after they took a poetry workshop together and developed a deep respect for each other's writing. King recalled, "I fell in love with her partly because I understood what she was doing with her work. I fell because *she* understood what she was doing with it. I also fell because she was wearing a sexy black dress and silk stockings—the kind that hook with garters."[4]

Stephen was a year ahead of Tabitha and graduated from the University of Maine in June 1970. Like many recent graduates, he soon discovered that his college degree did not guarantee him a job and a middle-class life. He moved into a rundown riverside apartment in Orono with little more than his battered Underwood typewriter. When he failed to land one of the few teaching positions available, he was forced to settle for menial labor, first as a gas station attendant and then at a commercial laundry

Did you know...

Stephen King was among the first undergraduates to ever teach a class at the University of Maine. Frustrated by the lack of attention his English classes paid to contemporary fiction, King proposed and developed a seminar called "Popular Culture and Literature." Though a professor officially led the class, King did most of the lecturing himself.

(an experience he later immortalized in a short story called "The Mangler.")

Tabitha and Stephen married in January 1971. By that time, they were already blessed with a little girl they named Naomi. Later that summer, Tabitha followed her husband into the "real world" and found a similarly bleak employment landscape. She took work at a Dunkin' Donuts, and the couple scraped by on their meager wages.

WHEN KING TO THE DARK TOWER CAME

In the late 1960s and early 1970s, the horror fiction market was in a slump. Most of the magazines and offbeat literary journals of the 1950s had faded away, leaving few places to publish. Those that survived paid pennies per page. As unlikely as it sounds today, the only magazines paying good money for scary stories were pornographic. King caught word of this trend and though not overly happy to have his work published between pictures of naked women, he had little choice.

The summer after graduation, those huge rats in the basement of the textile mill finally paid dividends when *Cavalier* magazine bought his story "Graveyard Shift" for $250. The following spring, King sold *Cavalier* another chilling tale called "I Am the Doorway." Both stories, and over a dozen more, would eventually appear in *Night Shift* (1977), King's first short story anthology. These collected tales inspired at least six feature films and a handful of television shows. At the time they were written, though, the money they earned barely kept the Kings off welfare.

King also began another novel about this time, inspired by the "spaghetti westerns" of director Sergio Leone and a classic poem by Robert Browning entitled "Childe Roland to the Dark Tower Came." King was curious about what might result if he dropped a gunslinger into a fantasy world. The story would ultimately expand into an epic series of books and earn King a whole new kind of readership. That too lay years in the future.

King was desperate for a break. He polished up *Getting It On* and submitted it to Doubleday after an editor there expressed some interest. The book bounced around the publisher's offices for a while, with various editors suggesting changes that King was all too willing to make. Just when it looked like a deal was going to be inked, Doubleday declined.

King was heartbroken. Bills were piling up and he was no longer able to convince himself that a writing career was just around the corner. He and Tabitha wanted to have more children, but how could they, under the circumstances? There was only one thing to do. He had to find a real job.

TEACHER'S BLUES

A position opened up at Hampden Academy, a school where King had been a student teacher while he was an undergraduate. Though he felt lucky to be steadily employed, the job was a mixed blessing. A steady paycheck totaling $6,400 per year may have slowed his slide into debt, but it also ate up almost all of his time to earn it.

To shorten Stephen's commute, the Kings rented a trailer in a town west of Bangor called Hermon. Between his duties as a teacher and a father, King somehow found a few hours every night to continue writing stories in a tiny room he shared with the furnace. He also completed yet another novel, entitled *The Running Man*. This too would go unpublished for some time, despite King's every effort to find a sympathetic publisher.

A photo of Hampden Academy in Maine, where Stephen King taught in order to support his family, while working on his writing at night.

Pressures began to mount. Their old Buick kept breaking down and there was never enough money to fix it. In an effort to offset costs, they had the phone company cut their service and rented out a room in their trailer to Steve's old friend Chris Chesley. Still, there were always more bills to pay than money to pay them. In the midst of all this, the Kings had another child. This time it was boy, whom they named Joseph. King was uncharacteristically terse about the strain this new addition put on the family: "He entered the world easily. For the next five years or so, nothing else about Joe was easy."[5]

As he now readily admits, King has always had difficulty drinking alcohol in moderation. He was overindulging as far back as high school. A trunk full of unpublished novels and a young family on the verge of welfare would push many men over the brink, and Stephen King was no different. It would take him years to admit it, but by this time he was a full-blown alcoholic.

A TREASURE IN THE TRASH

Drunk or sober, Stephen King always kept writing. He often credits his wife with keeping the faith during those tough times and never asking him to quit. She even excused his binge drinking to an extent. "Tabby was steamed about the booze, of course," King said in retrospect. "But she told me she understood that the reason I drank too much was that I felt it was never going to happen, that I was never going to be a writer of any consequence. And, of course, I feared she was right."[6] Tabitha King gave much more than moral support, though, when she rescued one of her husband's unfinished stories from the trash one day in 1972 and convinced him that it was worth finishing.

The story was an early version of what would ultimately become *Carrie*, King's first novel. He had been toying with the idea of a young girl whose telekinetic powers manifest at the onset of puberty, but the world of teenage girls felt foreign to him and the main character reminded him too much of (and was, in fact, named after) a girl from his youth who nobody liked. Would readers identify with the ugly duckling?

The other problem was the manuscript's length: it was too long for a short story and too short for a novel. King solved this by ingeniously padding out the page count with fake newspaper reports and other primary sources, giving his supernatural story the weight of truth, both literally and figuratively. Still, King had little confidence in his latest creation. "I thought who'd want to read a book about a poor little girl with menstrual problems? I couldn't believe I was writing it."[7]

Nevertheless, in early 1973, King submitted a draft to Bill Thompson at Doubleday, an editor who had liked but ultimately passed on his previous efforts. This time, Thompson was hooked. He suggested a few changes to the ending and King agreed with them. The manuscript made the rounds and everybody at Doubleday seemed to like it. Still, King kept his hopes in check. He had more immediate worries, anyway, as his family was on the verge of eviction from their trailer.

In March of that year a telegram arrived with the good news. Doubleday wanted to publish *Carrie* and was offering a $2,500 advance. The money may not have ended King's financial woes, but it did mean something equally important: He could continue writing.

A still from the climax of the Brian De Palma film adaptation of King's first novel, Carrie. Pictured, the actress Sissy Spacek, who played the troubled (and telekinetic) Carrie White.

3

The King of Horror Cometh

SAVED FROM DISASTER by the success of *Carrie*, the Kings packed up their things and moved to Bangor. They did not have to live in a trailer anymore, and they could afford a phone again, but $2,500 only goes so far. The majority of the money went toward buying a car that actually ran.

Two months later, on Mother's Day, 1973, even better news arrived. Bill Thompson called to say that Doubleday had sold *Carrie*'s paperback rights to New American Library (NAL) for a whopping $400,000 and King was entitled to half of it. Not only could they stop worrying about the phone bill, but now King could also quit his day job and follow what he truly believed to be his destiny. None of that sank in at the time, however. Still dazed and poor in his mind if not in actuality, King celebrated by going out to buy his wife a hair dryer.

"Creatively and financially, *Carrie* was a kind of escape hatch for Tabby and me, and we were able to flee through it into a totally different existence," he told Eric Norden in a 1983 interview for *Playboy*. "It was a great feeling of liberation, because at last I was free to quit teaching and fulfill what I believe is my only function in life: to write books. Good, bad, or indifferent books, that's for others to decide; for me, it's enough just to *write*."[1]

A NEW CHAPTER BEGINS

King completed the school year teaching at Hampden Academy and then moved his wife and children into a house on Sabago Lake, in southern Maine. By this time, he already had two more novels in the works. The first, entitled *Blaze*, was devoid of any supernatural elements. It told the story of a hulking giant of a man who, under the influence of an evil cohort and impaired by years of abuse as a child, ends up kidnapping a baby. King's other novel, titled *Second Coming* at the time, was a deliberate update of Bram Stoker's *Dracula*. Teaching the classic novel in his high school English class had inspired him to usher the vampire myth into the modern age and unleash it on a small, unsuspecting town.

Both King and Thompson agreed that *Second Coming* was the stronger of the two. In time, King changed the title to *Jerusalem's Lot* after the name of the town in which it takes place. This was also the title of a short story King wrote in college about a nineteenth-century family cursed by its association with a cult of the undead. Though the story provided a kind of historical backdrop for the novel, they bear little relation to each other, and, ultimately, the novel's title was shortened to *'Salem's Lot*.

AN OLD CHAPTER ENDS

Despite the unorthodox way in which she was forced to raise her sons, Stephen King's mother was an old-fashioned, independent New Englander. She may have depended on her sisters for help, but she certainly did not like to do so and did it only for the sake of her children. "There was a high premium on maintaining a pleasant exterior," King once remarked in an interview, "saying 'please' and 'thank you' even if you're on the *Titanic* and it's going down, because that was the way you were supposed to behave."[2]

This proud and stoic nature may explain why King's mother never told anyone she was seriously ill until it was too late. Perhaps she was tired of feeling like a burden. In any case, her doctors discovered uterine cancer in August 1973, just a few short months after her son finally broke through with *Carrie*. Had they known of her illness earlier, there may have been a chance to save her, but Nellie had kept the symptoms to herself. She lived only six months after she was diagnosed. As King put it, "I think [my mother] actually died of embarrassment."[3]

Both Stephen and his brother David were at her bedside when she died, and Stephen gave the eulogy at her funeral. By his own admission, he was drunk at the time. Later, he would pour some of his grief into a short story called "The Woman in the Room," which appeared in his *Night Shift* anthology in 1978.

CARRIE COMES OUT

The hardcover edition of *Carrie* appeared on bookshelves in the spring of 1974. It sold modestly well for a first novel, but few reviewers took notice. That would change soon enough. King had tossed his first pebble into the pond of popular culture, and the ripples were already beginning to radiate outward. They were felt as far away as Hollywood, where producers quickly recognized the novel's cinematic potential.

As several commentators have pointed out, *Carrie* is basically a retelling of the *Cinderella* story.[4] The evil stepsisters are like Carrie's cruel classmates who enjoy a normal social life while she stays home alone. The cold-ness of Cinderella's uncaring stepmother is mirrored in the insanity and religious fanaticism of Carrie's mother. There is even a fairy godmother of sorts in the character of Sue Snell, who feels bad enough for Carrie to lend the poor girl her boyfriend (Prince Charming) as a date for the prom (the ball), on the condition that it is for just one night (she must be home by midnight).

The key deviation is the ending: Neither Carrie nor any of her classmates live happily ever after. Fairy tales are, by definition, reinforcements of traditional values: prince gets princess, good triumphs over evil, and order is reestablished in the kingdom. In contrast, *Carrie* ends with anarchy and mayhem. In the process, King not only taps into the revenge fantasies of everyone who has ever felt like an outsider (foretelling the rise of crimes such as the shootings at Columbine), but he also deliberately addresses a hot topic of the era by empowering a young woman. "The book is, in its more adult implications, an uneasy masculine shrinking from a future of female

A photo of the cast of Stand By Me *(1986), a film directed by Rob Reiner which had been adapted from King's novella "The Body." From left to right, Wil Wheaton, Jerry O'Connell, Corey Feldman, and River Phoenix.*

equality," he writes in *Danse Macabre*. "Carrie White is a sadly misused teenager . . . but she's also Woman, feeling her powers for the first time and, like Sampson, pulling down the temple on everyone in sight."[5]

About the same time *Carrie* was published, Doubleday bought *'Salem's Lot* and subsequently sold the paperback rights to NAL for $500,000. In hindsight, it is clear that Doubleday took advantage of the situation by offering its new star author relatively small advances and then keeping 50 percent of the paperback proceeds, but at the time, King was too green and too happy with his newfound success to quibble over the contract. Instead, fueled by a newfound feeling of career momentum, he plowed straight ahead. In short order, he completed a novella, "The Body," and then another novel, *Roadwork*. The former's tale of four friends who set out on a morbid adventure would eventually appear in his *Different Seasons* collection and provide the basis for the hit movie *Stand by Me*. The latter concerns a man who takes a stand against developers and local officials intent on building a highway across his land.

In an afterword for *Different Seasons*, King famously described his books as "the literary equivalent of a Big Mac and large fries from McDonald's."[6] By 1974, Doubleday could already smell a franchise cooking and neither "The Body" nor *Roadwork* fit their conception of the menu, so they passed on them and awaited his next submission. Little did they know that King was about to enter one of the few rocky patches in his writing career.

THE SHINING

In late summer 1974, the Kings decided a change of scenery was in order and chose Boulder, Colorado, as their home away from home. On arrival, Stephen began work on "The House on Value Street." The infamous kidnapping of millionaire heiress Patty Hearst, who subsequently joined her abductors in their criminal crusade, dominated the headlines of the day. King was fascinated by the dynamics of a prisoner identifying with his or her captors (known in psychology as the Stockholm syndrome) and set about exploring the subject in his new novel. For whatever reasons, the book did not come to fruition and King abandoned it after a couple of months.

A classic story by Ray Bradbury called "The Veldt" served as the starting point for King's next project.[7] King was fascinated by the notion that something imaginary could manifest itself in real life—something frightening, of course, and something from the mind of a child. This was not just any child, but a child with paranormal sensitivity. This seed of an idea sprouted into a novel-in-progress that was initially called *Darkshine*. King knew that in order for the story to work, he must come up with a new twist on the haunted house cliché. Originally, he chose an amusement park as his setting. The problem with a haunted amusement park, King decided, is that if

Did you know...

Stephen King typically writes at least 1,500 words a day, six or seven days a week. Early in his career, he truthfully boasted that he only took off for Christmas and his birthday, but eventually that just became a stock answer to a question asked too often. He likes to work on something new in the morning, for about three hours. Later in the evening, he revises drafts of other works in progress and gets them ready for publication.

things become too scary, you have the ability to go home. To generate real fear, he needed a setting with no certain escape.

Fate stepped in and handed him a solution when he and Tabby took a weekend retreat at the Stanley Hotel, near Rocky Mountain National Park. They arrived the day before the hotel was to close for the season and soon discovered that they were the only guests. King spent the night in room 217, terrifying himself with visions of all the awful things that could happen to a family there, cut off from the outside world. Come morning, he had found the setting for his new novel. *Darkshine* became *The Shine* and, finally, *The Shining*.

However animated by the spirits of memory and history, a setting is just a stage. King needed characters to give his novel life. His first two novels had been partly inspired by people and places from his past: *Carrie*'s main character was an amalgamation of several outsiders he had known, both as a child and as a high school teacher, and the town in *'Salem's Lot* was largely modeled on Durham, the town of his youth. For his new book, King turned inward for the first time and projected aspects of himself onto the page. In many ways Jack Torrance is King's alter ego—a funhouse mirror in which all of King's own flaws and fears are magnified and multiplied. Torrance is a failure as a teacher, a writer, and a father. He is an alcoholic who teeters on the brink of madness. Mix in a psychic boy, a vulnerable wife, and a haunted hotel and King had all the ingredients for a horror masterpiece.

With each of his published novels, King was expanding his scope, examining horror on larger and larger scales. Both *Carrie* and *'Salem's Lot* are finite tales with clear beginnings and catastrophic endings. *The Shining* is a little more open ended. The book may have only had one true setting, a handful of characters, and an incendiary ending, but the stories behind the litany of evils associated with the Overlook Hotel stretch out in all directions like loose ends from a bag of yarn. The novel has both a prologue and epilogue, and both make it quite clear that the story does not begin or end with the Torrance family. Perhaps more important, King was improving his craft with each novel. Fellow horror writer Peter Straub read *The Shining* and concluded "[King] had made a huge leap in quality since *'Salem's Lot* and was now quite clearly one of the best writers of any kind in the United States."[8]

For his fourth book, King would employ his widest lens yet. His stage became America as a whole, and his cast of characters numbered in the dozens. This time the thing under the bed was no mere vampire or haunted house but the end of the world.

Pictured, the British author Peter Straub, at a benefit reading on February 2, 2002. Straub was an early admirer of King's work. Though opposite in temperament—Straub is reserved and intellectual, King is animated and brash— the authors have collaborated on two popular books, The Talisman, *a fantasy novel published in 1984, and its sequel,* Black House, *published in 2001.*

4

Riding the Ricochet

KING FINISHED A first draft of *The Shining* and then moved his family back to Maine in the summer of 1975. *'Salem's Lot* hit the shelves in hardback around Halloween of that year. The proceeds from his first two novels allowed Stephen and Tabby to buy their first house, in the town of Bridgton, near Portland.

When he wasn't working on a novel, King continued to write short stories—some were published at the time, others waited years to see print. On completion of *The Shining*, King dashed out "Apt Pupil," a novella about the evil bond that forms between a sociopathic boy and a former Nazi hiding in his town. Too long to be a story and too short to be a novel, "Apt Pupil" joined "The Body" and "The Running Man" in King's trunk of unpublished manuscripts. In time, all three would be made into movies, together grossing nearly $100 million. In 1975, King was still unproven in Hollywood, but that would change soon enough.

After a brief break, King began work on what would become *The Stand*. His abandoned novel "The House on Value Street" still occupied his thoughts, and, slowly, with the influence of random media snippets (a radio preacher talking about Judgment Day, a news story about a chemical spill), it evolved into something entirely different. What emerged was an epic story of good versus evil, set in the aftermath of a plague. King had already toyed with the idea of a "superflu" in an earlier story called "Night Surf," but now he filled in all the gruesome details: the rapid spread of the disease, the deaths of millions, and the collapse of society. King then polarized the survivors into two camps—the good go to Boulder, Colorado, and the evil head to Las Vegas, Nevada. The book's title promises a final confrontation, but, rather than pitting the opposing forces in physical combat, as in J.R.R. Tolkien's *The Lord of the Rings*, King concludes his tale with a Christian parable of sacrifice: Many are saved by the voluntary deaths of a few.

Although *The Stand* contains elements of the supernatural, it is not a horror novel in the traditional sense. Through its success, King was able to break free from the genre and earn himself the freedom to write any kind of book he pleased.

When he was finished, King's opus was well over 1,000 pages long, nearly twice the length of anything he had written before. Doubleday forced him to cut 150,000 words in order to lower production costs and the book's price. King realized that if he didn't make the edits himself, someone else would. When he was finished, he began searching for a way to wrest more control over both his finances and his intellectual property, but those crossroads lay a few years ahead. In the meantime, King would become a best-selling author and a Hollywood phenomenon.

BIG SCREEN BOOST

Already something of a local celebrity, King's popularity took a quantum leap when director Brian De Palma released his film adaptation of *Carrie*.

Twentieth Century Fox had bought the movie rights to the book in April 1974, shortly after its hardcover release. The project was tossed around Hollywood for a while until United Artists acquired it and De Palma signed on. The film was fairly low budget, even by prevailing standards. De Palma cast a group of largely unknown actors, including Sissy Spacek, John Travolta, and Amy Irving. The resulting film was a big hit, grossing over $30 million, thanks to strong performances, some striking camera work, and King's captivating story.

Released in November 1976, De Palma's film proved to be a fantastic promotional tool for the paperback edition of *Carrie* and helped it sell nearly one million copies in its first year in print. Sales of the hardback edition of *'Salem's Lot* received a boost, as well. King credits this "ricochet-action" as the main force behind his rise to fame.[1] Prolific King commentator George Beahm borrowed the phrase and further explained: "The ricochet effect—a hardback and a paperback reprint, followed by a movie—worked to great effect with King's books, since he was not only capable of producing a book a year, but also capable of writing in a cinematic style that translated easily to the screen."[2] Once set in motion, this effect would continue throughout King's career, earning him a huge income and the title of "horror's reigning monarch." New problems arose from his sudden ascendancy to the throne, though, which were practically unthinkable for a man who had been poor, unknown, and about to quit writing only a few years earlier. Could King be writing too much? Would the market become oversaturated with his books? Doubleday clearly thought so, which is why they could afford to pick and choose only his best books, leaving a well-stocked trunk of manuscripts that King felt were just as deserving of a spot on the shelf.

WRITING HIMSELF INTO A CORNER

Besides overexposure in the market, the other problem attending King's sudden rise to success was a newfound fame he neither wanted nor knew how to deal with. He

Did you know...

More than 30 motion pictures have been adapted from Stephen King's novels, novellas, and short stories. That's not even counting the dozens of television miniseries or short films. All told, these movies have brought in over a billion dollars in ticket sales. The highest grossing film thus far is *The Green Mile*, released in 1999, which made nearly $150 million.

found the limelight paralyzing. Now that he was a household name, he felt pressured to deliver another hit book, not only by his publisher, but also by a many-headed entity he began to call his "Constant Readers." Perpetual demands for interviews, book signings, and other appearances in the media were bad enough, but when obsessed fans began to descend on his home, King found himself looking for an escape hatch.

When King was stressed in the past, he could always escape into his writing; now the writing had become the source of the stress. He began work on a book called "Welcome to Clearwater" but hit a dead end. He started another novel titled "The Corner," but that, too, was abandoned. Next to nothing is known about either manuscript. A first stab at what would become *The Dead Zone* also failed to inspire him. Desperation began to sink in. He started a fourth novel about a little girl with the power to start fires telepathically, but worried that he was rehashing *Carrie*. "I had this depressing feeling that I was a 30-year-old man who had already lapsed into self-imitation," he told Douglas Winter, "and once that begins, self-parody cannot be far away."[3]

The only work King was able to finish during 1976 was a novella with the unwieldy title of "Rita Hayworth and the Shawshank Redemption." Like his other novellas, it had no market and was promptly filed away. In time it, too, would be published and eventually adapted into what is arguably the greatest "Stephen King" film ever made.

King has said "I had a bad year in 1976—it was a very depressing time."[4] The irony is that for any other writer, it would have been a *great* year. A popular movie came out based on his first book, *Carrie*, and he received a World Fantasy Award nomination for his second, *'Salem's Lot*.

Two more surefire winners, *The Shining* and *The Stand*, were already in the bag, just waiting to be published. By assessing such an envious position as "depressing," King revealed just how much pressure he felt at the time to live up to his hype.

SECRET AGENT MAN

The year 1976 was a crossroads year for Stephen King in more ways than one. Until that year, he had not thought much about acquiring an agent, even though it is standard practice for writers to have one. Although successful, he was not very savvy when it came to scrutinizing his contracts. Not only was Doubleday continuing to pay out paltry advances (less than $80,000 for his first five books[5]) and keeping half the proceeds from the sale of his paperback rights (which totaled nearly $2 million, after *The Shining* and *The Stand* were sold[6]), but they also had tricked their star author into a royalty agreement that gave him limited access to his own money. To lower his income taxes and perhaps as a hedge against lean years down the road, King had signed a contract which paid him $50,000 per year, regardless of how much he was owed. Doubleday would invest the rest of his earnings. His books generated so much revenue that this contract made it impossible for him to receive all of his royalties within his lifetime.

Needless to say, King was not happy with the situation. In 1976, he met Kirby McCauley, a young agent who quickly confirmed King's suspicions that he was getting a raw deal. King wasn't about to burn any bridges yet, but he did send McCauley on a trial mission of sorts—to help him find a wider audience for his short fiction. Before year's end, McCauley had delivered by getting a story called "I Know What You Need" into *Cosmopolitan* and another titled "The

A scene from The Shining, *a 1980 film adaptation of the King novel of the same name. Although King disapproved of the changes director Stanley Kubrick made, the film is considered a masterpiece of the horror film genre. Pictured in the foreground, the actor Danny Lloyd, whose character Danny Torrence has the ability to "shine"—or to see and communicate with the dead, including those twin girls at the end of the hall.*

Ledge" into *Penthouse*. Neither exactly qualified as the vanguard of literary publishing, but they were much more mainstream and lucrative than *Cavalier*.

BACK ON TRACK

The Shining was published in early 1977 and quickly became King's first hardback bestseller. Almost immediately, Hollywood came calling to ask for the film rights. Off to a good start, 1977 would only get better. His third child, Owen, was born in the spring. By the end of the year, King would sign a lucrative new contract, complete first drafts of three new novels, sell five more of his short stories, and launch the writing career of a mysterious man by the name of Richard Bachman.

King decided to give *Firestarter* another chance, realizing that "not only was it less like *Carrie* than I had thought—it was also better."[7] Charlie McGee, the heroine of his new novel, is considerably more sympathetic than Carrie White, not only because she is younger but also because she faces a greater foe. The villain in *Firestarter* is the American government. Charlie inherits her extraordinary powers as the result of an experiment conducted on her parents before she is born—both parents develop psychic powers that have mutated and are amplified in their daughter. The shadowy secret agency behind it all becomes aware of Charlie's talents, kills her mother, and imprisons her and her father in order to exploit them. The moral crux of the novel lies in the fact that in order to save herself and her father, a young girl must wield an evil power she cannot control.

A very similar problem lies at the heart of *The Dead Zone*, which King began first but finished at more or less the same time as *Firestarter*. On the eve of marrying his girlfriend, a schoolteacher named John Smith is rendered comatose after a bad accident. Five years later, he awakens to discover that the world he knew has moved on, including his girlfriend. Even worse, he emerges from the coma with the ability to foresee terrible events in the lives of those he touches. His "gift" is actually a curse, not only because these visions traumatize him and wreak havoc on his health and sanity, but also because they place upon him the dubious responsibility of trying to prevent something that may already be preordained. His predicament becomes significantly more desperate after Smith shakes hands with a presidential candidate and learns that the man will be responsible for starting a nuclear war. Smith sets out to assassinate him, but can he bring himself to follow through?

Late in the summer of 1977, with little publicity, a paperback book entitled *Rage* appeared on the shelves. Few buyers and even fewer reviewers decided to take a chance on an unknown author named Richard Bachman, and the book was promptly forgotten after its first print run. Meanwhile, Stephen King's Constant Readers remained desperate for something new to fill their insatiable appetite for his books. It would be another year before *The Stand* was available for consumption. Little did they know that their favorite author had recently taken a stand of his own.

Stephen King sitting on one of his motorcycles in front of the gates of his house in Maine.

5

While He Was Bachman

BACK IN 1972, before he had published his first novel, Stephen King was pinned with the label of "horror" writer. When he submitted a story called "The Fifth Quarter" that was more crime thriller than spooky chiller, *Cavalier* only agreed to publish it if King used a pen name. At the time, he was in no position to argue and chose "John Swithen." It turned out to be a one-time deal; John Swithen never appeared in print again.

Three novels later, each more successful and more frightening than the last, he was being heralded as the "King of Horror." Initially, he did not seem to mind the weight of the crown. His editor, Bill Thompson, who had read his earlier, non-horror novels, warned him after reviewing *The Shining*'s first draft that it would chain him forever to the genre. King was unfazed. "I thought about all the people who had been typed as horror writers, and who had given me such great pleasure over the years . . . . And I decided . . . that I could be in worse company."[1]

Nevertheless, all those unpublished novels and novellas must have haunted him, especially during that period in 1976 when it seemed like he had hit a dead end. In some ways, King was locked in the trunk with them—bound by what he considered to be an unfair contract with Doubleday and constantly pressured to deliver more of the same. *The Stand* was his first major attempt to break out. Doubleday recognized its greatness and bought the book, but only after forcing King to edit it down. King requested that a limited edition be published with the full text intact. Doubleday refused. This was the final straw, and King set about looking for another deal that would be both more lucrative and more liberating.

A NEW AMERICAN

Backed by his new agent, Kirby McCauley, Stephen King signed with New American Library (NAL) and its partner imprints, Viking and Signet. The contract delivered substantial upgrades in all respects. King received a multi-million dollar advance for *The Dead Zone*, a much more equitable share of the paperback rights, and, unbeknownst to everyone except a very select few, the power to secretly raise a few of his earlier books from the dead.

Resurrected first was *Getting It On*, the novel King had begun as a senior in high school and very nearly sold to Doubleday in 1971. King changed the title to *Rage* and chose "Guy Pillsbury" as his pseudonym. NAL rejected the name for fear that some astute reader would make the connection between King and the last name of his maternal grandfather. When pressed for an alternative, King scanned his office and lifted "Richard" from a novel by Richard Stark (which is actually a pseudonym for Donald Westlake) and "Bachman" from a record by Bachman-Turner Overdrive that was on his turntable.[2]

To prop up their puppet author and give him some stuffing, King and McCauley concocted a rudimentary life story for Bachman. They gave him a wife named Claudio Inez, a tenure in the merchant marines, a day job as a farmer, and a series of sympathetic tragedies: the drowning of his only child, a sick wife, and a midlife brain tumor. They even took a picture of McCauley's friend Richard Manuel and used it as the author photo. The ruse worked for a while but only because nobody was paying much attention. *The Long Walk* was published in 1979, followed by *Roadwork* in 1981, and *The Running Man* in 1982. All four Bachman novels failed to generate any buzz or sales. King attributes this to the lack of "fanfare" attending their release, but also insists "this was at my request; I wanted Bachman to keep a low profile."[3]

Nevertheless, rumors that Richard Bachman was actually Stephen King began to circulate in the publishing industry from the very beginning, forcing King to publicly deny the connection on more than one occasion. Despite his denials, King had left some tantalizing clues. *Rage* is dedicated to "Susan Artz and WGT": The former proofread *The Stand* and the latter are the initials of his editor, Bill Thompson. *The Long Walk* was dedicated to several of King's college professors. Other internal details, such as several fictional locations that crop up in both King and Bachman novels, threatened to give up the game. However, a game needs players and woefully few people even read the novels in their original printing, let alone caught wind of the elaborate hoax.

CANCER OF THE PSEUDONYM

Everything changed with *Thinner*, the fifth novel by Richard Bachman. The first four had no overt similarities to King's other books—nothing supernatural or grossly horrifying—and seemed to be the products of a struggling young man, filled with anger and a grimly pessimistic worldview. Given little promotion, they were quickly forgotten. Conversely, *Thinner* told the unmistakably King-like tale of an overweight lawyer named Billy Halleck who provokes the uncanny when he accidentally hits and kills a Gypsy woman with his car. Halleck's plush life is literally eaten away, pound by pound, under a curse cast by the Gypsy's

Did you know...

The saga of Richard Bachman has spawned persistent rumors that Stephen King has published novels under additional pseudonyms. Though there are others (including a hoax about an erotic novel), the two most often cited, according to Michael Collings, author of *Stephen King as Richard Bachman*, are a 1972 novel called *Exorcism* by Eth Natas (an anagram for "The Satan") and a sci-fi novel titled *The Invasion* by "Aaron Wolfe," published in 1975. King denies both claims, and for good reason: They are terrible books. *The Invasion* was actually written by fellow best-selling writer Dean Koontz.

father. Douglas Winter reports that *Thinner*'s prose was so glaringly similar to King's other books that one reviewer ironically dubbed it "what Stephen King would write like if Stephen King could really write."[4]

Upon publication in 1984, *Thinner* was actually advertised by a couple of savvy distributors under the name of its true author. The cat *really* clawed its way out of the bag, though, after an astute bookseller named Steve Brown performed a copyright search through the Library of Congress and discovered that someone at NAL had inadvertently put down Stephen King as the author of *Rage*. Armed with proof, Brown published an exposé in the *Washington Post*. Sales of *Thinner* skyrocketed, and, suddenly, everyone wanted to read the older Bachman novels, which were out of print by then. Signet rectified that in the fall of 1985 by issuing an omnibus collection called *The Bachman Books*. Written by Bachman, the novels sold modestly. Re-printed as "Four Early Novels by Stephen King," it was an instant best seller. King hardly needed any more proof that his name was, in and of itself, a bankable commodity.

Ever cognizant of his Constant Readers, King felt the need to explain his actions and did so in "Why I Was Bachman," an introductory essay for the omnibus edition. "I've been asked several times if I did it because I thought I was over publishing the market as Stephen King. The answer is no . . . but my publishers did."[5] The general rule in the publishing industry is that readers will only buy a certain number of books by their favorite author each year. Stephen King proved the exception and made the use of a pseudonym unnecessary. Nonetheless, King was upset about the premature end to his pet project. "I was pissed. It's like you can't have anything. You're not allowed to because you are a celebrity."[6]

DEMON DOGS AND DOLLAR BABIES

Beginning in the fall of 1977, eight years before the climax of the Bachman saga, King relocated his family to England for period a time. The plan was to rent a spooky old place and write a novel under its influence. That idea did not pan out, but the trip did afford King the opportunity to meet with fellow horror maven and *Ghost Story* author Peter Straub. Though worlds apart in temperament—Straub is reserved and intellectual, King is animated and brash—the men were great fans of each other's work, so when King proposed a collaboration, Straub eagerly agreed. It would take years for both men to clear their schedules and commit to the endeavor, but the partnership ultimately spawned *The Talisman*, a fantasy adventure novel published in 1984.

Instead of an English ghost story, King began a decidedly more real-world tale about a rabid dog that traps a boy and his mother in their car and terrorizes them over the course of three days and three hundred tense pages. King named the novel *Cujo,* after the dog, and published it in 1981.

The King family returned to Maine after a few months and bought a home in Center Lovell. Shortly thereafter, King realized his dream of securing a larger readership for his short fiction when Doubleday (to whom he stilled owed two books) published *Night Shift*, a collection of 20 stories spanning his career to the point. The passionate introduction King wrote for this collection clearly shows him still struggling with the stigma of the "horror writer" label, and the assumption that writing scary stories makes him not only a bad writer but also somewhat crazy to boot.

Even before *Night Shift* hit the shelves, film students and other amateur filmmakers had begun to write King and ask permission to make short films of his stories. King ultimately instituted an informal policy for dealing with such requests.

To the horror of his accountant, he granted blanket permission for the price of one dollar per adaptation, on the condition that he receives a copy of the film upon completion. In time, both these amateur films and the directors who made them became known as "Dollar Babies." All told, more than two-dozen Dollar Baby shorts have been made thus far. Among the first was "The Woman in the Room" by Frank Darabont. King liked it so much that he later granted Darabont the commercial rights for three major motion pictures (*The Shawshank Redemption*, *The Green Mile*, and *The Mist*).

BACK TO SCHOOL

Stephen King's career came full circle in the fall of 1978 when he accepted an appointment to teach at the University of Maine. *The Stand* was published just as the semester began, and the reputation of the university's new writer-in-residence soared.

King taught four classes over two semesters—two literature lectures and two writing seminars (fiction and poetry). In November, his friend and old Doubleday editor Bill Thompson proposed the idea for King to write a nonfiction book on "the horror phenomenon," as expressed in literature, film, and other media. The timing was perfect because King was already organizing his thoughts on the subject for a lecture course. King agreed to give it a shot and started work on *Danse Macabre* in the evenings, after his teaching duties were fulfilled.

Around the same time, King was struck by an idea for a new novel when his daughter's cat was killed crossing the busy road that skirted their property. They buried Smucky in an informal graveyard local kids had dubbed the "Pet Sematary" on a hand-painted sign. Idle thoughts about what might happen if the cat returned from the dead developed into the more horrifying idea of the same thing happening to a small child. King knew and loved the classic W.W. Jacobs story "The Monkey's Paw" and felt its classic premise of "be careful what you wish for" was ripe for a novel-length update. For the first time in his career, however, King questioned whether his "Imp of the Perverse"[7] had gone too far. As a parent, he found the whole topic almost too horrible to think about. He also knew intuitively that it tapped into a primal fear shared by anyone who has children. *Cujo* may have ended with the death of the boy, Tad Trenton, but it did not require King to "deal with the aftermath," as he once confided to Douglas Winter. "I have always been aware of the things that I didn't want to write about. The death of a child is one. . . . For me, it was like looking through a window into something that could be."[8]

Smucky was killed around Thanksgiving of 1978. Despite his misgivings, King completed a first draft of *Pet Sematary* by the following May. Drained by the experience, he put the manuscript in a drawer and tried to forget about it.

SPAWN OF DOLLAR BABY

King turned down an invitation to teach another year at the University of Maine, deciding to focus on what he did best. He returned to writing full-time in the summer of 1979 and kicked off an amazingly productive decade in which he would publish over 20 books and see many of them adapted for film or television.

Two books by King appeared that summer, but only one under his real name. *The Long Walk* became the second released under the Bachman pseudonym, but like *Rage* it failed to generate much interest. Readers were too busy devouring *The Dead Zone*. King's first Viking hardcover outsold *The Stand* by nearly three to one.[9]

Between continued work on *Danse Macabre* and *Pet Sematary* and a promotional book tour for *The Dead Zone*, King somehow found time to crank out both another novel and his first screenplay. The novel was titled *Christine* and told the very American tale of a teenage boy's love affair with his car. The twist was that this particular 1958 Plymouth Fury happened to be possessed. King also infused the book with his passion for classic rock-and-roll music, which he plays loudly while he writes as a kind of insulation against outside distraction.

Christine was not a standout novel for King in sales or acclaim, but it did mark the moment when its author stopped worrying about money and started thinking about his impact on the publishing world at large. Upon completing his new book, King sold *Christine* for a one-dollar advance, confident that he would make sufficient money on royalties. In doing so, he freed up millions of dollars that NAL could then use to support many other writers.

SHOCK TREATMENTS

Another first for King came in November 1979 when CBS aired a miniseries adaptation of *'Salem's Lot*, directed by Tobe Hooper (of *Texas Chainsaw Massacre* fame). The miniseries received mixed results. Restrictions on what could be shown on television at the time took some of the "bite" out of the vampire story, so to speak, but the series' four-hour running length allowed its writers to be much more faithful to the novel than would have been possible in a feature film.

Stanley Kubrick's treatment of *The Shining* proved to be the exact opposite. Released in June 1980, the film remains a cult favorite, mostly thanks to the strength of Jack Nicholson's manic performance, some very creepy visuals, and a nerve-wracking music score. King, however, was ambivalent. He enjoyed the film but disagreed with Kubrick's casting and decision to play down the book's supernatural elements. "What's basically wrong with Kubrick's version . . . is that it's a film by a man who thinks too much and feels too little," King told an interviewer. "That's why, for all its virtuoso effects, it never gets you by the throat and hangs on the way real horror should."[10]

King's first original screenplay, *Creepshow*, provided him with the opportunity to collaborate with *Night of the Living Dead* director George Romero. Conceived as a deliberate homage to the horror comics of their youth, *Creepshow* linked five separate tales within a loose frame story. Written in 1979 and not released until 1982, the resulting movie was almost universally panned by critics and audiences alike, though it did give its writer the chance to do some acting. Romero had used King once before, for the bit part of "Hoagie Man" in his 1981 movie *Nightriders*. For *Creepshow*, he offered his partner the much larger role of Jordy Verrill, a goofy farmer who falls victim to an unstoppable fungus after discovering a meteor in his field. Needless to say, it was not an Oscar-worthy performance, and King wisely kept his day job.

HOME HAUNTED HOME

King finished out 1979 as a co-guest of honor at the World Fantasy Convention with Frank Belknap Long, a friend and peer of the late horror master H.P. Lovecraft. King was humbled by the experience, in more ways than one. Numerous elder writers and influences of King's were present, and none of them had attained his level of success. At the convention, a small publisher named Christopher Zavisa pitched King with an idea for an illustrated calendar. King agreed, and, though the calendar project never panned out, King ultimately produced something more substantial in the illustrated novel *Cycle of the Werewolf*. Published three years later as a limited edition collector's item, *Cycle* was eventually reprinted as *Silver Bullet*, following the release of the film version in 1985.

In the summer of 1980, the Kings purchased a Victorian mansion in the historic district of Bangor. They kept their house in Center Lovell as a summer retreat, but the "William Arnold House" (as it was locally known, after the original builder) became an iconic emblem of the Stephen King empire, particularly after the Kings commissioned an architectural blacksmith to fashion a wrought-iron fence around the property, complete with bats, spiders, webs, and a three-headed dragon. There are even rumors of a resident ghost.

The Kings were wealthy enough to live anywhere they wanted, but their roots in Maine ran deep. "I think a place is yours when you know where the roads go," he once explained about their decision to live in Bangor. "They talk my language here; I talk theirs. I think like them; they know me. It feels right to be here."[11] King's connection with everyday American society is what makes his supernatural fiction so popular. He doesn't just write about regular Joes; he is one himself.

Shortly after moving to Bangor, King donated a large cache of his personal papers to the University of Maine for safekeeping, including the manuscripts of his three unpublished early novels: *The Aftermath*, *Sword in the Darkness*, and *Blaze*. In the years to come, the Stephen King collection at the university would continue to swell with the author's prolific output.

The October 6, 1986 cover of Time. *By the 1980s King was a household name and at the height of his powers, having sold millions of copies of his various books.*

6

Shifting into Overdrive

SOMETIME IN 1979, King began work on a new novel that would rival *The Stand* in scale and sheer storytelling prowess. "The book is a summation of everything I have learned and done in my whole life to this point," King boasted.[1] Told from multiple points of view and split over two parallel time frames, *IT* recounts the tale of six children who discover an ancient evil dwelling in the sewers of their town and return 25 years later as adults to face it again. King finished a mammoth first draft about a year later and then left the manuscript alone for a while to focus on other things.

FETE(S) FOR A KING

King received his first official accolade that year when the World Fantasy Awards honored him for "Special Contributions" to the field. Among those contributions was a novella called "The Mist," which served as the centerpiece both for *Dark Forces*, a horror anthology edited by his agent, Kirby McCauley, and for King's own *Skeleton Crew* collection.

In many ways, "The Mist" is the prototypical Stephen King story. It is the tale of a freak storm that traps ordinary people inside a supermarket, where they are tormented by an army of nightmarish monsters. King uses many of his trademark themes and plot scenarios: regular folk whose limits are tested by irregular circumstances, a familiar setting turned sinister, and the fallout of science that has gone unchecked. "The Mist" is also unusual among King's work in that it ends with the ultimate fates of its heroes left unknown.

King spent the first part of 1981 attempting to flesh out *Cycle of the Werewolf*, and that spring saw the publication of *Danse Macabre*. King's first nonfiction book earned him great respect among his peers, who recognized the book's author as not only a successful horror writer but also a true aficionado of the genre.

In 1981, Tabitha King published her first novel, *Small World*, which earned its author her own share of good reviews. She would go on to write three more novels in the 1980s alone, the majority of them set in the fictitious Maine town of Nodd's Ridge.

Principal shooting for *Creepshow* began in May. His son, Joe, who also played a small part in the film, joined King on the set. To entertain himself during breaks, and under the campy influence of the movie, King reworked an earlier idea about a bunch of characters trapped in an apartment building who end up eating each other.[2] The story proved too unsavory—even for its author—and remains unpublished.

The hardcover edition of *Cujo* hit the bookstores in October and continued King's streak of instant best sellers. The third Bachman novel, *Roadwork*, appeared as a paperback original around the same time. King humbly accepts some of the blame for its lackluster sales, calling it "the worst of the lot, simply because it tries so hard to be good."[3]

Despite his failed pseudonym experiment, King no longer had reason to fear that his writing was only getting recognized for its ability to sell books and scare people. In 1981, King received a World Fantasy Award nomination for "The Mist," and a Nebula Award nomination for "The Way Station" installment of his ongoing serial novel, *The Dark Tower: The Gunslinger*. He also earned a British Fantasy Award for his contributions, to match the one bestowed in 1980 by his American cohorts. The following year, *Danse Macabre* earned a Hugo Award for Best Non-Fiction Book from the World Science Fiction Society. Although no doubt gratifying, these awards all came from his peers within the horror and fantasy fields. The prize that most likely meant the most to him was a Career Alumni Award from the University of Maine. King had come a long way from student to teacher to honored guest. Seven years later, Stephen and Tabitha both received honorary doctorate degrees from their alma mater.

A CHANGE IN THE WEATHER

When King first began writing, the novella format was not a viable commodity. Few magazines could spare that much ink, and book publishers knew from experience that they simply did not sell. For most authors, this is still true today.

Stephen King, however, is unlike most authors. Time and time again throughout his career he has wielded enough commercial force to change the publishing landscape. All told, he has put out three collections of novellas so far (four, if you count *The Bachman Books*). Not only has each and every one become a best seller, but they have also inspired a host of excellent films.

The first, considered by critics to be his best, is *Different Seasons*. For this book, King dusted off three earlier novellas, "Rita Hayworth and the Shawshank Redemption," "Apt Pupil," and "The Body," and wrote a brand new one titled "The Breathing Method." His fans proved loyal, whatever format he chose to write in, and snapped up more than 140,000 copies of the collection in hardcover alone.[4] All four novellas are largely based in reality and generate their wondrous power, suspense, and chills with nothing more than good old-fashioned storytelling.

TARGET MARKET PRACTICE

Christine and *Pet Sematary* were both published in 1982. When it came time to decide which book to put most of his promotional efforts behind, King chose the former. There were two main reasons for this choice. The first was related to the contractual conditions under which *Pet Sematary* was published. Doubleday was still withholding royalties from his earlier books and parceling out the $50,000 per year, as stipulated by his old contract. King cut a deal to get the rest of his money. Doubleday wanted two more books, but he gave them *Pet Sematary* and called it even.

In addition to lacking the desire to fill the coffers of his ex-publisher, King still harbored fears that *Pet Sematary* was simply too dreadful. In the lone interview he gave on the subject, King admitted that writing it had been "a gloomy exercise" in the hard-core realities of death and grief and that it was the one book he refused to reread. "I never want to go back there again, because it is a *real* cemetery."[5] Ironically, especially in light of its plot, King's attempt to bury the book gave it a morbid life of its own. Word got out that it was too scary, even for its author. *Pet Sematary* sold nearly 700,000 copies in hardcover alone and garnered King some of his best reviews to date. In contrast, *Christine* sold many fewer books and received enough critical derision to convince King that he must have been wrong about its merits.

Similarly off the mark was King's commercial assessment of *The Gunslinger*, the first book in his epic "Dark Tower" series. Begun over a decade earlier, and serialized over several years by *The Magazine of Fantasy and Science Fiction*, this masterful blending of genres was completely unlike anything he had previously written. The action is set in a parallel universe, both otherworldly and eerily familiar, and the plot revolves around an antihero named Roland of Gilead, who begins the tale tracking a mysterious man in black. Despite ample proof that his Constant Readers would follow wherever he led, King had his doubts about how many of his mainstream fans would tag along. "I didn't think anybody would want to read it," he later told an interviewer.[6]

A specialty publisher named Donald Grant convinced King otherwise and offered him a chance to reward his most loyal fans with a beautifully produced keepsake. Plans were made for a lavish edition with color illustrations. The original print run was small and only advertised in trade magazines and small press catalogs. Nonetheless, word spread quickly within the tightly knit fantasy community and every single copy sold. King thought that would be the extent of it.

King's uninformed Constant Readers were very unhappy when they opened their copies of *Pet Sematary* and saw a book titled *The Dark Tower: The Gunslinger* listed among those by their favorite author. Why hadn't they heard of this book before? Where could they buy it? A sudden demand flared up, but by that time *The Gunslinger* was a collector's item and copies—when found at all—were selling for five times their original price. King authorized a second print run of an additional 10,000 copies, but

Did you know...

Looking for a tax write-off and the opportunity to liven up the AM dial with some of his favorite rock-and-roll music, Stephen King bought an ailing Bangor station on Halloween in 1983 and dubbed it WZON. King sold it several years later, but then reacquired it in 1993 when the station went bankrupt. Today, WZON focuses on broadcasting local sporting events.

that wasn't nearly enough, especially after the same thing happened four years later with the release of the sequel, *The Dark Tower II: The Drawing of the Three*. King had deliberately issued the books as limited editions to prove that he was "not entirely for sale—that [he was] still in this business for the joy of it."[7] Torn between a desire to stay true to his word and an almost compulsive need to please his Constant Readers, King would eventually relent in 1988 and allow NAL to produce trade editions of the books with large print runs. In the meantime, however, King continued to experiment with small publishers and break free of expectations.

EXPERIMENTS SMALL AND LARGE

With sales of his novels skyrocketing, King spent much of 1983 and 1984 seeking out projects that would bring him back down to earth and keep him connected with the less commercial segments of the industry. Contemporary with King's limited-edition experiment with *The Gunslinger* was another, even smaller project called *The Plant*. King set up his own publishing operation, called Philtrum Press, and enlisted a college friend to help him design and print a unique gift for the 200 close friends and family on his Christmas list. Instead of a card, King sent them a comic horror novel-in-progress about a small publisher who falls afoul of a mad botanist after rejecting his manuscript for publication. Originally, only three installments of *The Plant* were thus distributed (in 1982, 1983, and 1985), but, 15 years later, King would publish additional segments in a whole new format (see Chapter 10).

King's next small-press book was a limited edition of *Cycle of the Werewolf*, published in 1983 by Land of

Enchantment and complete with pen-and-ink drawings and watercolor plates. Though gorgeously produced, the various editions were sold at prices exorbitant enough for King to threaten legal action. In the end, he simply repackaged the book two years later, renamed it *Silver Bullet*, and included his screenplay for the film adaptation along with the complete text of the original.

Despite his popularity with the general public, King could never quite convince his daughter Naomi to read any of his books. In early 1983, when Naomi was 13, King began writing a new book he hoped might change her mind. Lavishly published a year later by King's own Philtrum Press, *The Eyes of the Dragon* was as much a work of art as it was a classic fairy tale. King privately distributed the book at Christmas in lieu of his annual installments of *The Plant*. Needless to say, his daughter was not the only one enchanted. Viking released a trade edition of the book four years later.

King's obvious love of fantasy carried over into his next project as well. Conceived in 1977 and written over the following seven years, *The Talisman*, his collaboration with Peter Straub, was finally published in October 1984. Interestingly, it resembled neither of their previous works. A boy named Jack Sawyer sets out on a quest to save his mother, who is dying of cancer. In order to do so, he must pass into a parallel universe known as the Territories to find a magical artifact. Although the Territories have narrative ties to the world of *The Dark Tower*, the majority of King's fans had yet to read that growing series and therefore did not make the connection. As a result, the reaction to *The Talisman* was lukewarm and befuddled. Reviews were unenthusiastic; most focused on the novelty of two authors, and failed to recognize the book's narrative grandeur. Nevertheless, *The Talisman* was a huge commercial success and topped the best-seller lists for an amazing 28 weeks.

BOX OFFICE BLUES

On paper, at least, *Creepshow* should have been an easy home run. For horror fans, having George Romero direct an original screenplay by Stephen King seemed like a dream come true. Even the anthology format of the film gave them five chances to connect. Unfortunately, the resulting film produced nothing but errant foul balls. Despite the effective, if occasionally inaccurate, adaptations of *Carrie*, *'Salem's Lot*, and *The Shining*, successfully translating King's words into quality viewing has proven to be the exception and not the rule, at least as far as his horror material is concerned.

This isn't to say many haven't tried to adapt King's work. Between 1983 and 1986, a staggering eight feature films were based on his books. *Cujo*, *The Dead Zone*, and *Christine* appeared in the summer of 1983. Of the three, only *The Dead Zone* earned any critical praise, thanks in large part to the skill of director David Cronenberg and a haunting performance by Christopher Walken. *Firestarter* and *Children of the Corn* followed in 1984. *Firestarter* was intended as a big-budget blockbuster, starring Hollywood heavyweights George C. Scott, Martin Sheen, and Louise Fletcher, as well as a young Drew Barrymore, fresh from her starring role in *E.T.* Loosely based on a story from the *Night Shift* collection, *Children of the Corn* was the exact opposite: a low-budget effort that used largely no-name actors and lacked any input from King. Both were box office bombs.

In 1985, *Cat's Eye*, a slightly more respectable anthology film based on another original King screenplay, was released, together with the utterly forgettable werewolf flick, *Silver Bullet*.

Why did horror fans, who snapped up King's books so readily, stay away from these film adaptations? In hindsight, it appears that many of the filmmakers were more interested in cashing in on King's name than making worthwhile movies. People began to joke about what the next "Stephen King Movie of the Month" would be.

King himself stepped into the fray in 1986. Following the old adage that "if you want something done right, do it yourself," he agreed to direct *Maximum Overdrive*, a film about big rigs with bad intentions based on "Trucks," another story from *Night Shift*. Because King had no experience as a director, and the movie hinged on one of the least plausible plots he had ever constructed, the resulting film was more schlock than shock. Even a rocking soundtrack by AC/DC failed to draw much of an audience.

Fortunately, 1986 also saw the release of another film that not only ended King's streak of flubs, but also exposed his storytelling talents to a much wider audience. Adapted from King's novella "The Body" (from *Different Seasons*), *Stand by Me* struck a major chord with baby boomers who had grown up with King during the 1950s (the time in which the film was set), and also with adolescents who could easily relate to its timeless tale of four boys on an intrepid adventure. One of those baby boomers was the film's director, Rob Reiner, who identified so much with the fictional small town in which the story was set that he subsequently named his production company

Castle Rock Entertainment. In the years to come, Castle Rock would produce numerous acclaimed films based on Stephen King books.

Stephen King in 1986. Although highly successful, King would find that his addiction to drugs and alcohol would almost ruin his career. An intervention spearheaded by his wife, Tabitha, would help him get clean and sober.

7

Personal Demons

THE STEPHEN KING Express was heading for a crash, but the only people who knew it were those in his immediate family. To all outward appearances, the engine was running full steam ahead, just as it always had. *Skeleton Crew*, King's second collection of short fiction, was published in the summer of 1985 and went on to become one of the best-selling anthologies of all time. The following summer, *Stand by Me* was delighting moviegoers. The omnibus edition of *The Bachman Books* followed in October. That same month, *Silver Bullet* was released and King appeared on the cover of *Time* magazine.

Faced with abundant proof that King's readership was virtually insatiable, NAL and Viking decided to throttle up the publication of books he had already written. Four new Viking hardbacks hit the shelves in a little more than a year, starting with the unveiling of *IT* in October 1986 and ending with the November 1987 release of *The Tommyknockers.* Bookended between them were a new edition of *The Eyes of the Dragon* and *Misery,* a novel originally slated to be the fifth published under the Bachman pseudonym.

IT ARRIVES

Big books and the high profile authors who write them often make easy targets for critics. At nearly 1,200 pages, and with an initial print run of one million copies, *IT* lumbered onto the publishing scene like a white elephant with a bright red bulls-eye painted on it. Many reviewers deemed it overlong and sloppy and chastised its author for what they considered to be a lack of discipline. King, however, considered it among his best novels ever. His loyal fans agreed and made the book a mammoth hit.

The Eyes of the Dragon was more elusive prey. Set in the same mythical Territories where *The Talisman* takes place and featuring the return of *The Stand*'s arch villain Randall Flagg, the book manages to be both playfully irreverent and unapologetically traditional at the same time. Some of King's Constant Readers shied away from its fairy tale aspects, but on the whole those who did buy a copy (at least 500,000 in the first year alone) were rewarded with a timeless story that spoke as much to adults as it did to King's thirteen-year-old daughter, Naomi.

King followed up *The Eyes of the Dragon* with the limited edition release of *The Dark Tower II: The Drawing of the Three.* The *Dark Tower* sequel made it clear that an epic series was developing: It sold out as fast as the first, leaving the vast majority of his fans empty-handed. King knew he had to rectify the situation, but he wanted to do so on his own terms.

MISERY LOVES COMPANY

The rocky marriage between Stephen King and his Constant Readers hit a midlife crisis with his fifteenth novel. *Misery* is the story of Paul Sheldon, an author of best-selling romances that feature a heroine name Misery Chastain. Sheldon wants to focus on writing literary fiction instead, so he kills off Misery in one final installment. Shortly thereafter, he crashes his car in a snowstorm. To the rescue comes a mentally deranged woman named Annie Wilkes, claiming to be Sheldon's "number one fan." Wilkes kidnaps Sheldon, holds him prisoner, and forces him to bring Misery back to life.

Misery turned out to be everything *IT* was not: short, taut, and completely believable. The novel earned its author his best reviews in years, as well as a bag full of angry letters from his Constant Readers, who felt the character of Annie Wilkes was an obvious parody of them.

They were right of course, but only to a certain extent. Any reader unhinged enough to identify with the demented Annie Wilkes probably deserved, and perhaps even benefited from, the look in the mirror that the novel provided. What such readers failed to understand, however, is that King was writing about more than just the lunatic fringe of his fandom. Annie Wilkes was also an amalgamation of all the pressures that were weighing on King at the time, including those that came from within. Writing for him had always been as much a compulsion as a career choice—an innate need to tell stories and have them heard. "The more

I wrote," King told one interviewer, "the more I was forced to examine . . . why I was doing it and why I was successful at it; whether or not I was hurting other people by doing it and whether or not I was hurting myself."[1]

THE INTERVENTION

How could King have been hurting himself and others by writing books? One answer lay in a secret long kept from his fans. "By 1985 I had added drug addiction to my alcohol problems," he candidly admits in his memoir.[2] Both habits were deeply intertwined with his writing routine, and King feared that he would not be able to keep up without them.

His wife, Tabitha, organized an intervention in which family and friends confronted King and forced him to admit he had a problem. Tabitha kicked things off by dumping a trash bag full empty beer cans, drugs, and drug paraphernalia taken from his office onto the rug in front of him. King stalled and lied to himself, but eventually came to his senses. "What finally decided me was Annie Wilkes, the psycho nurse in *Misery*. Annie was coke, Annie was booze, and I decided I was tired of being Annie's pet writer."[3]

KNOCKING THE KNOCKERS

King's next novel, *The Tommyknockers*, was written in the spring and summer of 1986, during the height of his substance abuse. The plot concerns a buried alien spaceship that exerts a strange influence on the citizens of a nearby town. "What you got was energy and a kind of superficial intelligence . . . What you gave up in exchange was your soul. It was the best metaphor for drugs and alcohol my tired, overstressed mind could come up with."[4] When *The Tommyknockers* was published in November 1987,

Stephen and Tabitha King at the fifty-fourth Annual National Book Awards Ceremony in New York City. Married since 1969, the fellow writers have supported each other throughout their careers.

reviewers panned it as subpar material, without focus or any compelling characters. Not a surprise, considering King's state of mind as he was writing it.

Other commercial and critical failures that year included two movie sequels: *Creepshow 2* and the straight-to-video *Return to 'Salem's Lot*. The first had King's support (and another cameo). The second did not. Both were cheap knockoffs, but a big budget was not necessarily the answer to King's ongoing box office failures, as proven by *The Running Man*, another film released in 1987. With Arnold Schwarzenegger miscast as the victimized hero and expensive special effects overshadowing the story line, the film failed to earn what it cost to make.

DERAILED

Deprived of the drugs and alcohol that had kept his writing engine greased and fueled, The Stephen King Express ground to a halt in early 1988. For only the second time in his career, King checked his tank and found it empty. To make matters worse, NAL had drained their reserve of unpublished King works, leaving nothing new to print except a photo book called *Nightmares in the Sky* that contained a long essay by King. When this book proved insufficient to fill the demands of King's Constant Readers, NAL agreed to release a trade edition of *The Dark Tower: The Gunslinger*. In the fall of 1988, fans everywhere were finally given the chance to accompany Roland of Gilead on his enthralling quest. The sequel was also released in trade paperback the following spring.

For his part, King contends that he "never stopped writing" during this period, only that what he wrote wasn't worth publishing. "Little by little I found the beat again, and after that I found the joy again. I came back to my family with gratitude, and back to my work with relief."[5]

FIELD OF SCREAMS

Ever since watching Don Larsen of the New York Yankees pitch a perfect game in the 1956 World Series, Stephen King has been a huge baseball fan. Newly clean and sober, he decided to take a more active role as a father and become more than just a spectator. In the spring and summer of 1989, King helped coach his son Owen's little league team, the Bangor West All-Stars, to a state championship. King's involvement solidified his reputation with the locals as a regular guy with deep ties to his community. Several years later, King would strengthen those ties by donating more than one million dollars to build Bangor a new ballpark, known locally as the "Field of Screams." In the interim, King chronicled the championship season in a 1990 essay called "Head Down" that shocked the literary establishment by appearing in the rarefied pages of *The New Yorker* magazine. This essay surprised readers who previously had been unwilling to admit King's talent.

MAINE MAN (AND WOMAN)

Elsewhere, King and his family were finding other ways to give back to their home state. When film producers approached him with the desire to adapt *Pet Sematary*, he insisted that it be shot in Maine. After all, the state had given him more than just a place to live; its people and their steadfast way of life were inextricably woven into his books and stories. His trademark way of rooting his supernatural tales in the soil of regular life came straight from the people he observed and interacted with every day. Forcing Hollywood to come to Maine not only injected millions of dollars into the local economy, it also lent the movie a level of realism that was lacking in too many of the previous efforts. As a result, *Pet Sematary* succeeded at both selling tickets and scaring the audience.

Another successful film adaptation was *Misery*. For the film version, King again partnered with *Stand by Me*'s director Rob Reiner. Reiner's deft direction helped make the movie a big hit with both audiences and critics. Kathy Bates's masterful portrayal of Annie Wilkes earned an Academy Award. *Misery* not only showed future filmmakers how to tailor King's works to film, it also ushered in a period of consistently higher-quality adaptations. Sure there continued to be one cut-rate stinker released for every "Ste-

Did you know...

Tabitha King is equally as philanthropic as her husband. In 1991, she donated $750,000 and much of her own time to help build the Old Town Public Library, creating a truly first-rate community resource. Several years later, the Bangor Public Library received more than three times that amount from the Kings to help in its own renovation project. The local YMCA, various medical centers and schools, and a local swimming complex have also benefited greatly from the Kings' generosity.

phen King" film worth watching, but the ones that did work went a long way toward saving his good name.

BACK ON TRACK

King's so-called period of "writer's block" lasted barely six months. In truth, it only merits mention because of the personal crisis that attended it and his amazingly prolific output before and after. By February 1989, King had already signed a new contract which promised his publisher four new books in short order.

First up was *The Dark Half*, published in late 1989. Appropriately enough, it involved another writer in peril, but instead of a psychopathic fan, the author-hero Thad Beaumont must confront and vanquish a murderous alter ego. As with *Misery*, King's real-life struggle gave *The Dark Half* its frighteningly believable edge. The following May, Doubleday finally released a "Complete and Uncut Edition" of *The Stand* with all of King's original text intact. Both books received rave reviews from critics and fans.

Four Past Midnight arrived in August 1990. None of the tall tales comprising King's second collection of novellas exceeded the high standard set by *Different Seasons*. Nevertheless, both the critics and the buying public deemed them worth reading well into the wee hours. For many, the best in the collection was "Secret Window, Secret Garden," another King riff on the theme of the writer versus himself.

Stephen King performs with his band, the Rock Bottom Remainders, on November 14, 2000 in Denver, Colorado. The band, made up of famous fellow authors, including Amy Tan, Barbara Kingsolver, and Matt Groening, donate the proceeds from their concerts to charity.

8

Risk and Reward

STEPHEN KING'S THIRD decade as a writer was every bit as fertile and productive as the two that preceded it. He continued to take risks with regard to the genre, format, and subject matter of his creations. Some of these experiments failed, and others were great successes. Unfortunately, the 1990s also began and ended with two experiences as terrifying as anything in his books.

In April 1991, a schizophrenic man named Erik Keene broke into the Kings' home in Bangor and accosted Tabitha King with the news that he was carrying a bomb. King's wife, who was home alone at the time, managed to escape unharmed.

The police later captured Keene in the attic of the house and took him back to Texas, where he was imprisoned. As troubling as the incident was, Keene made it even worse by vowing to return, should he ever be let out.

CASTLE ROCK CURTAIN CALL

The fictional town of Castle Rock has served as the setting for a number of King's books and stories, including *The Dead Zone*, *Cujo*, "The Body" (*Different Seasons*), "The Sun Dog" (*Four Past Midnight*), and *The Dark Half*. In the fall of 1991, Viking published *Needful Things*, a novel King announced would be the last of the Castle Rock stories. "It's easy to dig yourself a rut and furnish it," King explained at a press conference. "After a while, I started to feel excessively comfortable in Castle Rock—I don't think that's a good state for a novelist to be in."[1]

The title of this final Castle Rock novel is taken from the name of a new store in town, opened by a stranger named Leland Gaunt. In this store, the people of Castle Rock find the objects of their deepest desires. Some of these "needful things" are ordinary but rare, like an autographed baseball card; others have magical qualities, like a necklace that cures arthritis. In exchange for these items, Gaunt does not ask for money but instead for a favor. The favors are seemingly innocent tricks or pranks, played at the expense of someone else in town. Slowly but surely, Gaunt's store and its irresistible inventory undermine the moral foundations of Castle Rock, turning good people bad and inducing betrayal and death.

Earlier that year, King had released the limited edition of *The Dark Tower III: The Waste Lands*. By year's end, the trade paperback edition was out and available to anyone who wanted a copy. It had been four years since the last installment, but it turned out to be worth the wait. The third book in the series mapped many of the murky edges of King's epic creation, beguiling readers with a fully realized fantasy world and a cast of characters as vivid, strange, and sympathetic as any that had come before. The "Dark Tower" books were escapist fiction, in the best sense of the phrase, for both King and his readers. Writing them required him to step away from his familiar haunts, like Castle Rock, and venture into unknown terrain. To reproduce that exhilaration outside of the "Dark Tower" series, King would have to find additional ways to break the mold and challenge himself.

IN THE PATH OF THE ECLIPSE

King's next two novels both explored the subject of abused women, though from different vantage points. In *Dolores Claiborne*, King tells the story of a foul-mouthed old woman accused of one murder, who ends up confessing to another. It is unlike any of his other books in that it is told in one, long, first-person monologue, without chapter breaks or shifts in point of view. This technique builds momentum and suspense and gives readers no convenient place to break.

Gerald's Game took risks as well. King had previously kept his books "PG-13" with regard to explicit sex. His new book, however, starts off with Jessie Burlingame and her husband experimenting with sexual bondage in a remote cabin in the woods. The "game" goes bad and Gerald dies of a heart attack, leaving Jessie still handcuffed to the bed. The rest of the novel is set in that same bedroom. The only additional characters are a stray dog and a phantom presence that may or may not be imaginary. Writing a good novel is hard enough, but restricting himself to one character and a one-room setting was sort of like King restraining both himself and his readers to those shackles with Jessie. The result for many reviewers and fans was claustrophobic and intense, but not particularly enjoyable.

Three years later, King again explored the theme of abuse with *Rose Madder*, a novel about a woman named Rose Daniels who suffers years of physical and emotional battering at the hands of her husband. Rose decides to run away, and finds not only temporary happiness in an unnamed city but also a magical painting that transports her to the otherworldly realm of King's "Dark Tower" mythos. When her husband finally tracks her down, Rose is able to trap him in this other world, where he meets a gruesome end.

Each of these novels proved less popular than the last. In fact, *Rose Madder* was King's first book in years not to

Did you know...

Dolores Claiborne and *Gerald's Game* were initially conceived as a two-volume set, to be called *In the Path of the Eclipse*. The books are linked by the fact that major events in each (Dolores' murder of her husband, and Jessie's rape by her father) both occur during the same solar eclipse of 1963. This gives the principal characters a kind of "psychic sisterhood" and a brief window into each other's lives. King ultimately chose to downplay the connection, however, and published the books separately.

hit number one on the *New York Times* best seller list. His Constant Readers, it seems, were not as interested in risky stories about victimized women as they were in King's trademark thrills. Fortunately for them, King also released *Nightmares & Dreamscapes* during this period, his third and largest collection of short fiction to date.

ROCKIN' OUT

When King isn't pushing the envelope with his writing, he is often busy promoting personal causes and enjoying other hobbies. Over the years, one of his pet crusades has been the fight against censorship. The conservative political climate in the 1980s and early 1990s gave rise to a number of religious and civic groups seeking to limit access to books and other media they deemed offensive or "pornographic," and that often included books by Stephen King. In 1986, King was instrumental in striking down a referendum in his home state that would have wrested the choice of what to read from the people and put it in the hands of the government. Six years later, in May 1992, King attended "A Celebration for Free Expression" during an annual convention hosted by American Booksellers Association. On the program that night was a very special appearance by a rock-and-roll band called the Rock Bottom Remainders (a "remainder" is a book sold at deep discount to cut losses from over-ambitious print runs). Conceived as a one-time lark, the Remainders were comprised of several best-selling authors, including Amy Tan, Barbara Kingsolver, Matt Groening (of *Simpsons* fame), and Stephen King. A handful of professional musicians were also on board to help keep everyone in tune and on key.

Those in attendance who expected a gag performance were pleasantly surprised to discover that these writers had enough chops to get the joint jumping, including King on guitar. Playing music had been a passion of King's since his childhood. He had even hopped on stage to jam with the band at his prom, but seldom, if ever, had he played in public since that night. By all accounts, the Rock Bottom Remainders were a huge hit at the convention. A revolving cast of members has reunited many times since then to give encore performances, including a mini tour for charity in 2007.

MORE HITS AND MISSES, AND ONE HOME RUN

Adapting King's work to the big screen continued to be a risky proposition—not that this stopped or even slowed the ever-growing number of hit seekers lining up on deck. Fortunately, for every outright failure, such as *Creepshow 2* (1987) or *Graveyard Shift* (1990), there were decent films worth watching, including *The Dark Half* (1993), *Needful Things* (1993), and *Dolores Claiborne* (1995).

The same proved true of the small-screen treatments. On the whole, if King wrote the teleplay, as he did for the miniseries adaptations of *IT* in 1990 and *The Stand* in 1994, the results were generally quite good. If he did not, such as in *The Tommyknockers* in 1993 and *The Langoliers* in 1995, then the results were mediocre. It helped, of course, when the original novel was a winner to begin with. Those who tried turning short stories into miniseries or full-length movies fared the worst. *Graveyard Shift* (a 1990 film), *Sometimes They Come Back* (a 1991 miniseries), *The Mangler* (a 1995 film), and *The Lawnmower Man* (a 1992 film) all rank as some of the worst "Stephen King" productions ever. The last one was so bad, and so unlike its source material, that King successfully sued to have his name completely disassociated with it.

A movie still from The Shawshank Redemption, *a 1994 film directed by Frank Darabont and starring Morgan Freeman* (left) *and Tim Robbins. Adapted from the novella "Rita Hayworth and the Shawshank Redemption," it is one of the most critically acclaimed film versions of a Stephen King work.*

The critical and commercial successes of *Stand by Me* and *Misery* suggested that the sweet spot for potential movie projects lay in King's novellas and shorter novels. Long enough to tell a two-hour tale, yet short enough to maintain interest and be faithfully reproduced, these two movies were also largely devoid of the supernatural elements that pass through a reader's imagination but tend to look hokey on film. In 1994, a previous "Dollar Baby" director named Frank Darabont took those lessons to heart when he wrote and directed *The Shawshank Redemption*, a fantastic movie starring Tim Robbins and Morgan Freeman. *The Shawshank Redemption* went on to earn seven Oscar nominations and a spot on the American Film Institute's list of the 100 best American films of all time. King and Darabont have teamed up twice since then, for *The Green Mile* in 1999 and *The Mist* in 2007. They also have plans to adapt *The Long Walk* sometime soon.

KING THE CARTOGRAPHER

Stephen King's novels have several points of geographic intersection, from which his story lines radiate like roads from a roundabout. One of them is Castle Rock; another is the city of Derry, which King based on Bangor and used as the setting for *IT*. Derry also appears in *Pet Sematary*, *The Tommyknockers*, and half a dozen other books. The third is the parallel universe in which the "Dark Tower" books are set, as well as the Dark Tower itself, which turns out to be a kind of inter-dimensional hub. As discussed here and in previous chapters, *The Stand*, *Rose Madder*, *The Talisman*, and *The Eyes of the Dragon* all contain textual links with King's fantasy series, whether they are characters, settings, or more obscure references. In 1994, King published *Insomnia*, a novel that built an interchange between Derry and the Dark Tower and hinted at the possibility that a big road atlas exists somewhere in King's mind and that he is capable of mapping his body of work as a whole. The primary narrative of *Insomnia* is about a man named Ralph whose inability to sleep causes hallucinations that convince him shadowy forces are at work behind what we know as reality. In the course of telling Ralph's tale, King expands the "Dark Tower" mythology and explains many of its underlying concepts. Unfortunately, all of this philosophical complexity proved too heady for all but King's most devoted fans, and *Insomnia* became one of his few books that many readers put down unfinished.

In 1997, King turned 50. Most writers in his situation would settle for more of the same, following whatever formula had earned them success and fame in the first place— but Stephen King is unlike most writers. With energy and imagination to burn, King would in the years to come not only devise new and innovative ways of hooking his readers, but he would again change the rules of what makes a best-selling book. It would take a head-on collision to halt the flow of stories forever pouring from his head, and even that would only silence him for a short time.

The author holding a copy of his book at a cocktail party honoring Storm of the Century, *King's first miniseries written directly for television.*

9

To Hell and Back

STEPHEN KING HAD earned the adulation of readers world-wide. Hundreds of millions of his books had been sold, with more than their fair share turned into films or television programs. He lived in a big house, had several nice cars, got to play in a rock band every now and again, and could afford box seats to watch his beloved Boston Red Sox play any time he wanted. What he still didn't have was the respect of academics and of so-called "serious" writers and readers who equated his mass-market appeal with bad writing.

Little by little, though, King managed to convince a few inhabitants of the Ivory Tower to come down and read his writing. Among the first were the editors of *The New Yorker*, who had published "Head Down," his nonfiction piece about coaching Little League. Four years later, the magazine again honored King by featuring his short story "The Man in the Black Suit" in their Halloween issue. The piece caught the attention of William Abrahams, longtime editor and judge of the O. Henry Awards, an annual compilation celebrating the year's best short stories. Abrahams shocked the literary world by not only selecting King's story, but also awarding it first prize. Best-selling authors are not supposed to be among our literary giants, at least according to those who consider themselves the authorities on such matters, but once again Stephen King proved to be the exception to every rule put before him.

THE GREEN MILE

King broke the rules again in 1996 by serializing his next novel, *The Green Mile*, into six thin paperback installments, publishing one per month. What some saw as a gimmick, others recognized as a conscious return to the "cliffhanger" radio programs and pulp magazines of King's youth, as well as to nineteenth-century Victorian novels that were first serialized in monthly magazines before being published as a single volume. The story about an old prison guard's magical encounter with a huge but simple-minded Death Row inmate captivated just about everyone who read it. By the time the last installment arrived, Stephen King's books were occupying an unprecedented six spots on the *New York Times* best-seller list *at the same time*. After such a feat, readers would have been able to forgive him if he decided to take a rest, but he was just getting started.

TERROR TWO PACK

To a casual observer, it might seem like Stephen King takes an almost maniacal pleasure in testing the limits of his readership. Would they buy a book in six installments? Absolutely. Fine, but would they buy two huge books simultaneously, one by King and one supposedly by the deceased Richard Bachman, each featuring the same cast of characters, but telling completely different tales and resulting in different outcomes?

Armed with this premise, King released both *Desperation* and *The Regulators* in the fall of 1996. NAL wanted to credit King as the real author of *The Regulators*, but he held his ground and Bachman got the byline. In the end, the point was really moot. Over a million copies of each book appeared in bookstores on the same day. Thanks to a lavish promotional campaign, it was impossible to mistake *The Regulators* for anything but a Stephen King book. Both novels promptly joined the six installments of *The Green Mile* on the best-seller list.

ONE STEP FORWARD, ONE LOOK BACK

Following his eight-book blitz in 1996, King scaled back somewhat for 1997. With the exception of the limited-edition release of *Six Stories* (a collection containing the prize-winning "Man in the Black Suit"), the only King book released that year was *The Dark Tower IV: Wizard and Glass*.

Fans of the series had waited six long years, so instead of causing an uproar, King decided not to limit the print run of the special edition hardcovers and even agreed to sell them in the chain bookstores. He further appeased the masses by providing those who did not want to pay for the hardcover with a trade paperback edition later in 1997 and a mass-market paperback in 1998.

Early in 1997, King also orchestrated a television mini-series remake of *The Shining*. In presenting a more faithful adaptation of the novel, King hoped to fix everything he felt was wrong with Kubrick's version. Director Mick Garris even managed to secure permission to shoot the series inside the real Stanley Hotel that had inspired the book. Though a few fans and critics enjoyed the update, the majority found King's version poorly acted, stylistically bland, and simply not frightening. If anything, it only served to prove that what works on the page may not always work on the screen.

FISHING FOR BONES

King spent the remainder of 1997 writing a major new novel called *Bag of Bones*. The plot involved a successful author struggling with grief over the death of his wife, a bad case of writer's block, and the growing realization that either his summerhouse is haunted or he is losing his mind. To many fans and reviewers, it sounded like a retread of books like *Misery* and *The Dark Half*. To some extent it was, but for King and many other writers, certain themes or story lines are like favorite fishing holes. Regardless of how many whoppers King has reeled in from that body of water, there is always the one that got away—that perfect fish hiding at the bottom, waiting for the right words to make it surface. Consequently, King keeps returning to that water, using different bait, casting his line from new vantage points.

The business behind the publication of *Bag of Bones* suggests that this time King felt he had come home with a very big fish. Apparently unhappy with a number of marketing decisions by NAL, as well as the huge deals they were offering to other authors such as Tom Clancy, King broke with his longtime publisher for the second time in his career. Instead of negotiating a new deal in private, he took the bold step of having his business manager auction off *Bag of Bones* to the highest bidder. In the short term, this created a lot of bad publicity. Many people both inside and outside the industry felt King was just being greedy. In the long term, King's gambit netted him greater control over how his books were marketed and published, as well as a larger share of the royalties. In the end, he signed a three-book deal with Scribner, a well-respected subdivision of Simon & Schuster.

For his part, King took this opportunity to disappear for a while. He flew to Australia, grew a beard, bought a Harley-Davidson motorcycle, and rode it across the outback. Clearly, he needed to recharge. On his return from a similar trip 10 years later, King explained: "One of the reasons I went to Australia . . . was to purge my head, or at least try. I wanted a month away from everything, partly to get rid of the clutter, mostly to see how things would look when I got back."[1]

OUT OF THE STORM AND INTO THE WOODS

The vacation in Australia kicked off a little break from the publishing spotlight, at least in Stephen King terms. *Bag of Bones* was his only book to appear in 1998. Nevertheless, his gamble with its publication had paid well, earning him his biggest sales to date and his first mostly favorable reviews from literary critics who had long disregarded his work. The following year found him again trying to squeeze his Imax-sized imagination onto the little screen when he wrote and helped produce *Storm of the Century,* a miniseries for ABC. This time around, he had greater success, both in terrifying his audience and in scaring up some good reviews.

King also scored big with his next book, *The Girl Who Loved Tom Gordon*. This short novel, about a nine-year-old girl who gets lost in the woods while out hiking with her mother and brother, pulled all the right strings, from its proliferation of baseball metaphors to its dead-on depiction of a neglected child's magical thinking. It was also his first book since *Eyes of the Dragon* fit for a younger audience.

Published in September 1999, King's next book, *Hearts in Atlantis*, was a collection of loosely interlinked novellas and short stories that earned him considerable praise and a few more converts from the literary camp. In 2000, he published a combination memoir and treatise, *On Writing*, which he had begun in late 1997. He finished the memoir section and was just about to tackle the more difficult part, on what makes for good writing, when disaster struck: He set out for a walk on June 19, 1999. He came home three weeks later, nearly 50 pounds lighter, pieced together with metal pins, and lucky to be alive.

THE ACCIDENT

The impact broke King's right leg in nine places. It also left him with a broken hip, four broken ribs, a spine riddled with chips, a collapsed lung, and a gaping head wound that required two dozen stitches to close. Emergency medical technicians arrived quickly and saved King's life. Over the course of multiple surgeries, an orthopedic surgeon succeeded in reconstructing his leg, but it took nearly a year of intense physical therapy before he could walk again.

It's easy to make too much of the fact that Stephen King's stories and novels feature an inordinate number of evil vehicles and vehicular mishaps. He had, in fact, recently completed the first draft of *From a Buick 8*—in which the main character's father is killed by an oncoming car—when the same thing very nearly happened to him. For his part, King says that he does not feel there is any connection. "I only use those things in my stories because cars and traffic accidents are a part of our lives, they are something that, unfortunately, most of us relate to. . . . It's a part of the American experience . . . but I never felt that I had jinxed myself."[2]

THE AFTERMATH

King was back at work several weeks later, trying to finish *On Writing* from a wheelchair, but he could barely sit for an hour before the pain became intolerable. Though his body healed little by little, additional surgeries and a severe infection in his punctured lung left him weak and depressed.

Did you know...

The driver of the van that hit King died from an overdose of pain medication a little over one year later, *on King's birthday*. After his accident, King asked a friend to buy the van, so it wouldn't end up on eBay or in the hands of some morbid collector. Rumors persist that King then took a sledgehammer to it, but in fact it met a less dramatic demise in the jaws of a car compressor.

After struggling so hard to get clean, he was now hooked on painkillers.

Nevertheless, King soldiered on. In March 2000, he experimented with a new way to reach readers by selling an "e-book" called *Riding the Bullet* via download from his Web site. To spread the word, the file was free for the first week. Unfortunately, hackers broke the encryption on the file and ruined King's plan by disseminating the book over the Internet. In hopes of preventing the same problem, King implemented an "honor system" with his next attempt. Eight years before the pioneering rock band Radiohead did the same with their album *In Rainbows*, King offered digital installments of his old serial novel *The Plant* for free, hoping readers would buy it later if they liked it. The program was met with only limited success, however, and King discontinued it in December, after six installments.

The first print novel published after the accident was *Dreamcatcher*, which he wrote longhand in bed to avoid sitting on his battered hip. A bloody and fast-paced blend of *Aliens* and *Invasion of the Body Snatchers, Dreamcatcher* may not be among King's best novels, but it did signal a return to the kind of visceral horror lacking in more literary efforts like *Bag of Bones* and *Hearts in Atlantis*.

King then reunited with old pal Peter Straub to write a sequel to *The Talisman*. Set decades later, *Black House* finds Jack Sawyer, the young hero of the first book, retired from his job as a homicide detective and repressing memories of his boyhood odyssey in the Territories. Gruesome murders force Jack back into action and across the boundary between parallel worlds.

Finished for the most part before his accident, *From a Buick 8* appeared in 2002. King revealed in the Author's Note that the first draft had taken him just two months to write, which may explain why many critics felt this retread of *Christine* reads like it was written by an author on cruise control.

It also explains why early in 2002 King announced in an interview with the *Los Angeles Times* that he was giving up writing. "You get to a point where you get to the edges of a room, and you can go back and go where you've been and basically recycle stuff . . . or say I left when I was still on top of my game."[3] King promised five more books, including *From a Buick 8*, another collection of short fiction called *Everything's Eventual*, and the remaining three volumes in the "Dark Tower" series. "Then that's it. I'm done." Was he really, though? Perhaps he just needed something to get excited about—like maybe his favorite baseball team winning the World Series.

King receiving the 2003 Medal for Distinguished Contribution to American Letters at the National Book Awards.

10

The Comeback King

IN THE AFTERWORD to *The Gunslinger*, the first volume of the "Dark Tower" series, King writes about his feeling at the project's outset that something monumental was in the works, "that it was time to stop goofing around with a pick and shovel and get behind the controls of one big great God a'mighty steam shovel, a sense that it was time to try and dig something big out the sand."[1] He also laments that "at the speed which the work entire has progressed so far, I would have to live approximately 300 years to complete the tale of the Tower."[2]

With his own mortality thrown into stark relief by the accident, and fearing (prematurely, it turned out) that his well of creativity was running dry, King got back behind the controls of the steam shovel in 2002 and set about finishing what he had begun. *The Dark Tower V: The Wolves of Callah* was published in 2003. Up to that point, he was averaging five or six years between volumes, but King cranked out the remaining two volumes, *The Dark Tower VI: Song of Susannah* and *The Dark Tower VII: The Dark Tower*, in a little more than one year.

Reviews of the entire Dark Tower series are as varied as the people who write them. Some consider it equal to anything imagined by J.R.R. Tolkien or Frank Herbert, the author of the *Dune* series. Others thought that the last couple of installments were mired in too much mysticism and squandered the momentum generated by earlier books. For his part, King was happy with the series and for having reached the end of a long and arduous writing journey.

In October 2005, King signed a deal with Marvel Comics to release a prequel comic book of the Dark Tower series called *The Gunslinger Born*. Though King has not had a direct hand in their creation, the comics, which focus on Roland's early years, have proved extremely popular. More recently, J.J. Abrams, creator of the television series *Lost*, has expressed an interest in bringing the Dark Tower series to the big screen.

THE PRIZE

Late in 2003, Stephen King completed another kind of quest: That year, the National Book Foundation awarded him a medal for Distinguished Contribution to American Letters. Never before had an author so popular with the masses or writing outside the genre of "literary fiction" been so honored. Certain academics criticized the decision and said it represented "another low in the shocking process of dumbing down our cultural life," to quote a vocal King opponent.[3] Others felt it was long past time to quit marginalizing so-called "genre writers" and admit that a good story is a good story, regardless of subject matter or style. Millions of readers worldwide obviously agreed with the latter view.

King spent the majority of his acceptance speech crediting his success to the undying support of his wife, Tabitha. The remaining portion he devoted to singing the praises of other critically slighted "horror writers" like Peter Straub and Jack Ketchum, as well as all those who came before him and never received the recognition they deserved. "My message is simple enough," he concluded, "We can build bridges between the popular and the literary if we keep our minds and hearts open."[4]

THE POP OF KING

One opportunity for King to build such a bridge came courtesy of *Entertainment Weekly*, which offered him the chance to reprise the role of pop culture commentator from his "King's Garbage Truck" days by writing a monthly column on whatever struck his fancy. Taking a soft jab at Michael Jackson, he called it "The Pop of King," but that was the last punch he pulled. "These are things I actually care about," he says in his debut column. "Consequently, I will not be cute, dismissive, patronizing, or indulgent. I may make you angry—I hope I do make you angry—but I will not waste your time."[5] A longtime victim of critical sniping, King soon proved he could dish out picks and pans with the best of them.

KINGDOM COME

Just because he had supposedly stopped writing novels did not mean King was done frightening people. Film and television adaptations of his work continued unabated, including a six-season series based on *The Dead Zone*, TV remakes of *Carrie* and *'Salem's Lot*, films versions of *Dreamcatcher* (2003) and *Secret Window* (2004), and numerous other projects. In 2004, King also developed his longest-running miniseries to date, adapting *Kingdom Hospital* from a similarly titled Danish miniseries that was originally directed 10 years earlier by pioneering filmmaker Lars von Trier. *Kingdom Hospital* ran for 13 episodes, but failed to reach the creepy depths or tap into the twisted humor of the original.

LIFTING THE CURSE

Fans of the Boston Red Sox and Stephen King's Constant Readers have at least one thing in common—they stay loyal. Sure, they may complain and grumble and take a kind of twisted pride in the lack of respect their fanaticism earns them from the world at large, but no matter how many disappointing seasons or mediocre books come and go, both groups are die-hard.

Despite his 2002 promise to quit writing, King decided in 2004 to display his longstanding dedication to his favorite baseball team the best way he knew how—he would write a book about it. Drawing on personal diaries and e-mail exchanges, King and fellow novelist Stewart O'Nan chronicled the entire season, from spring training all the way through to the miraculous comeback in the American League Championship Series against their archrivals, the New York Yankees. (Back in 1919, a year after they had won their last World Series title, the Red Sox traded the legendary Babe Ruth to the Yankees and then promptly fell under what became known as the "Curse of the Bambino," a curse that supposedly kept the Sox from winning another

World Series.) In 2004, after losing the first three games to the Yankees in the playoffs, the Sox rallied to win the final four games of the series—a feat no other team had ever accomplished in major-league history. That story alone would have been enough material for a great sports book, but when the Sox went on to win their first World Series in 86 years, it seemed almost fitting that a writer known for his deft touch with the supernatural was on board for the ride. King and O'Nan's book, *Faithful: Two Diehard Boston Red Sox Fans Chronicle the Historic 2004 Season*, was published in 2005 and went on to win a Quill Award for best sports writing. Currently, there are plans to turn the book into a miniseries for HBO.

DABBLING IN CRIME

There's no doubt King was revitalized by the success of his beloved Red Sox, but he wasn't quite ready to return to his old ways. Not yet, anyway. In 2005, he gave a small press called Hard Case Crime the opportunity to publish his first mystery novel, *The Colorado Kid*. King has always been a voracious reader, with tastes that range from highly literary to pulp trash, and hard-boiled crime thrillers are among his favorites. Instead of trying to match the masters, King decided to write a relatively "soft-boiled" and philosophical novel in which the central mystery never gets solved. Once again, reviews were polarized. Some felt cheated and hated it. Others were charmed by King's characters and the pragmatic realism of an ambiguous ending.

BACK FROM THE DEAD

Readers disappointed by King's detours into sports and crime writing were rewarded in 2006 with his first major horror novel in five years. *Cell* is vintage King, turning something as omnipresent and seemingly benign as a cell phone (which King refuses to use, by the way) into a vehicle for apocalyptic mayhem and terror. Horror fans everywhere breathed a sigh of relief; there was life enough left in the aging spookmeister to still scare their pants off.

That same year, King also produced *Lisey's Story*, a sort of sister novel to *Bag of Bones*. Having already broken his promise to stop writing, King felt little compunction repopulating the allegedly abandoned town of Castle Rock, where a writer's widow named Lisey Landon finds much more than dust bunnies in the dark corners of her husband's study.

King completed his string of resurrections and reversals by once more raising Richard Bachman from the dead in 2007. The pseudonymous alter ego emerged from his premature burial with a book called *Blaze* that King had written back in 1973. How Bachman managed to spirit the original typed manuscript from the special collections at the University of Maine is anyone's guess, but at least he did it for a good cause. All the author's proceeds from the sales of *Blaze* go toward supporting The Haven Foundation, a nonprofit charity that King established in 2006 to help support writers, illustrators, and other freelance artists who are unable to work due to disease or injury.

In June 2007, King joined the company of such literary giants as Truman Capote (*Breakfast at Tiffany's*) and Norman Mailer (*An American Dream*) when *Esquire* magazine published his novella "The Gingerbread Girl" in its entirety. The tale may not have jump-started the short fiction industry, as *Esquire* intended, but it certainly sold a lot of magazines and further confirmed King's acceptance into the club of "serious" writers.

King's latest novel, as of this writing, is *Duma Key*, published in early 2008. Though others have touched on the same subjects, this book is the first by King to make the psychological effects of injury and the redeeming power of art its central plot devices. The main character is Edgar Freemantle, a building contractor who loses his right arm in an accident on the job. Unable to work or control his bouts of rage, he becomes depressed and suicidal, especially after his wife leaves him. Only the rediscovery of an old talent for painting and a move to the gulf coast of Florida keep Edgar from going off the deep end. This is a Stephen King book, after all, so the deep end is always lurking only one misstep away and nothing good comes without a price. In addition to a newfound zest for life, Edgar's acts of creation awaken an ancient evil that seeks to use him for its own nefarious purposes.

Did you know...

In August 2007, King was mistaken for a vandal when he nonchalantly walked into a bookstore in Australia and began signing copies of his books. The store management initially failed to recognize King, who had not given any advance warning of his visit. King was apparently gracious about the error and most of the signed books were subsequently sold for charity.

A mid-1980s photo of Stephen and Tabitha King at their home with their three children: Owen, Naomi, and Joseph. Both sons are now published authors; Naomi is a minister in the Unitarian Universalist Church.

The idea of a human being acting as a conduit for some supernatural force, lacking control or understanding of the very power that gives his or her life meaning, is a central motif that runs throughout almost all of King's books, from *Carrie*, *Firestarter*, and *The Dead Zone* all the way through *The Dark Half* and *Duma Key*. Clearly, it is King's metaphor for the act of writing, something he was unable to stop doing despite it being physically painful for him to do after his accident.

ALL IN THE FAMILY

As it happens, Papa King is not the only family member destined for the writing life. Tabitha King had set off down that path long before they met in college; their marriage derives much of its lasting power from having that thread in common. As mentioned briefly in Chapter 6, Tabitha published four novels in the 1980s and three more in the 1990s. In 2006, her collaborative novel with horror writer Michael McDowell, *Candles Burning*, proved she was still at the top of her game. Though often overshadowed by her husband's works, Tabitha's books have earned her the respect of fellow fantasy and sci-fi luminaries such as Harlan Ellison.

On several occasions, Stephen King has confessed to the belief that he inherited both his creative mind and its dark bent from his absentee father. If there is such a thing as the "storytelling gene," then both King parents have passed it on to their children. Their eldest son, Joe, began writing at an early age, just like his father. His stories also had a creepy edge, also like his father's. When it came time to submit them professionally, Joe refused to take the easy route. He wanted his work to stand on its own merit, so he decided to leave off his last name, truncate his middle, and submit his work under the byline of Joe Hill (a nod to the early labor leader, after whom he was named). For nearly 10 years, not even Joe's agent knew his true identity. *Variety* magazine revealed the family connection shortly before the release of Joe's acclaimed supernatural thriller, *Heart-Shaped Box*, in 2007. By then, no one could say he had made it on anything but his own talent.

Joe's younger brother, Owen, is also proving to be a chip off the old block. After earning a master's degree in fine arts from Columbia University, Owen went on to publish a collection of stories in 2005 called *We're All in This Together*. Though he has never hidden his parentage, Owen has also earned his own way by writing in a more literary, reality-based style than his father.

Stephen and Tabitha's firstborn, Naomi, also tells stories, but from a pulpit instead of a paperback. After graduating in 2005 from the seminary at the Meadville Lombard Theological School in Chicago, Naomi went on to become a minister in the Unitarian Universalist Church. She currently leads the congregation of a church in South Florida, a few hours from where the Kings now own a waterfront mansion.

GHOSTS OF THINGS YET TO COME

Sometime in 2000, while King was still recuperating from his accident, country-rocker John Mellencamp approached him with the idea of collaborating on a musical, called *Ghost Brothers of Darkland County*. King, who had always admired Mellencamp's earthy songs about everyday people, immediately agreed, but the project took a long time to materialize. Signs of progress were whispered about in the trade magazines every couple of years, but there was never any definitive proof. According to *Billboard* magazine, however, the project is no longer just a figment of the imagination. *Ghost Brothers* is set to open in April 2009 at the Alliance Theatre in Atlanta, with a script by King and music by Mellencamp. The plan is to road test the production on smaller stages before making a bid for Broadway. There's no word about King braving the stage himself, but, given his penchant for surprises, one never knows.

King recently teamed up with *The Shawshank Redemption* director Frank Darabont to adapt his classic novella, "The Mist." Many aficionados considered it the best horror film of 2007. The pair has plans to adapt *The Long Walk* to the screen as well. Half a dozen additional film projects are also in the planning stages, including adaptations of *The Talisman*, *Bag of Bones*, *Cell*, *Black House*, *The Girl Who Loved Tom Gordon*, *From a Buick 8*, and a remake of *IT*.

However these film adaptations turn out, Stephen King has clearly earned a place in the starting lineup of America's greatest storytellers. With each new trip to the plate, he adds to his legacy, and, regardless of how he performs in any individual at-bat, he can be certain of one thing: A legion of fans will be roaring from the stands.

CHRONOLOGY

1947   Born September 21 in Portland, Maine.

1949   Father abandons the family and is never seen again.

1949–1958   Bounces around the country with his mother and brother, living with various relatives.

1958   Settles in Durham, Maine, to live in the house of his maternal grandparents.

ca. 1959– 1960   Finds box of his father's books, including a collection of stories by H.P. Lovecraft.

1962–1966   Attends Lisbon Falls High School; writes his first original stories and a short (unpublished) novel called "The Aftermath"; helps his older brother David publish an amateur newspaper.

1965   First story published ("I Was a Teen-Age Graverobber").

1966   Graduates from Lisbon Falls High School; enrolls at the University of Maine at Orono; completes *The Long Walk*.

1967   Publishes "The Glass Floor" in *Startling Mystery Stories*; begins work on *The Sword in the Darkness* (unpublished novel).

1968   Completes *The Sword in the Darkness*, which is rejected by 12 different publishers; publishes several more short stories.

1969   Meets Tabitha Spruce; writes "King's Garbage Truck" column for the college paper; publishes three more short stories.

1970   Graduates from UMO; daughter, Naomi, is born.

1971   Marries Tabitha and takes a job teaching at Hampden Academy; completes *Getting It On* and very nearly sells it to Doubleday; publishes two more short stories.

1972   Son, Joseph, is born; completes *The Running Man*, but cannot find a publisher; begins *Carrie* as a short story and later expands it into a novel.

1973   Mother dies of cancer; Doubleday's purchase of *Carrie* and subsequent sale of paperback rights allows King to stop teaching and write full-time; writes *Blaze* (unpublished until 2007); completes *Second Coming* (later re-titled *'Salem's Lot*).

1974 Completes *Roadwork*; writes first draft of *The Shining* after moving to Boulder, Colorado; begins work on what ultimately becomes *The Stand*; continues to publish short stories; *Carrie* is published.

1975 Completes draft of *The Stand*; moves back to Maine; publishes *'Salem's Lot*.

1976 Abandons two unfinished novels; film version of *Carrie* is released.

1977 Publishes *The Shining* and *Rage*, the first Bachman book; finishes drafts of *The Dead Zone* and *Firestarter*; son, Owen, is born; temporarily relocates to England and meets Peter Straub; writes a draft of *Cujo*; returns to Maine and buys a house in Center Lovell.

1978 Begins teaching at the University of Maine in Orono; publishes *The Stand* and *Night Shift*.

1979 Switches publishers; completes drafts of *Christine, Pet Sematary*, and *Danse Macabre*; writes *Creepshow*, his first screenplay; publishes *The Dead Zone* and *The Long Walk* (as Richard Bachman).

1980 Buys historic mansion in Bangor; completes first draft of *IT*; donates first cache of personal papers to UMO; *Firestarter* published; World Fantasy Award for "Special Contribution" to the field.

1981 *Danse Macabre, Cujo*, and *Roadwork* (as Bachman) are published; multiple awards and nominations.

1982 Begins *The Talisman*, in collaboration with Peter Straub; Hugo Award for *Danse Macabre*; *Creepshow* is released; publishes *The Dark Tower: The Gunslinger, Different Seasons, The Running Man* (as Richard Bachman) and several short stories.

1983 Completes drafts of *The Talisman, The Tommyknockers*, and *Eyes of the Dragon*; publishes *Christine, Pet Sematary*, and *Cycle of the Werewolf*; film versions of *Cujo, The Dead Zone*, and *Christine* are released; buys a radio station, WZON.

1984   Writes *Thinner* and *Misery*, as well as the screenplay for
Silver Bullet; publishes *The Talisman* (with Straub), *Thinner*
(as Bachman) and a limited edition of *The Eyes of the
Dragon*.

1985   Writes screenplay for *Maximum Overdrive* and temporar-
ily relocates to North Carolina to direct it; *Cat's Eye* and
Silver Bullet films released; publishes *Skeleton Crew* and *The
Bachman Books*; appears on the cover of *Time* magazine.

1986   Publishes *Silver Bullet* (repackaged edition of *Cycle of the
Werewolf*) and *IT*; two more films based on his works are
released: *Maximum Overdrive* and *Stand by Me*; family
stages alcohol and drug intervention; King starts to get clean.

1987   Publishes *Misery*, limited edition of *The Dark Tower II:
The Drawing of the Three*, Viking edition of *The Eyes of
the Dragon*, and *The Tommyknockers*; *Creepshow 2* and *The
Running Man* hit the big screens.

1988   Has writer's block; collaborates on photography book with f-
stop Fitzgerald called *Nightmares in the Sky: Gargoyles and
Grotesques*; releases trade edition of *The Dark Tower: The
Gunslinger*.

1989   Trade paperback edition of *The Dark Tower II: The Drawing
of the Three*; limited edition releases of *Dolan's Cadillac* and
My Pretty Pony; film version of *Pet Sematary* released; *The
Dark Half* is published; helps coach his son Owen's team to
a Maine State Little League Championship (and chronicles
the experience for *The New Yorker*).

1990   Doubleday unveils the unabridged edition of *The Stand*; *Four
Past Midnight* published; *Graveyard Shift* and *Misery* movies
released; *IT* miniseries airs on ABC.

1991   Limited edition of *The Dark Tower III: The Wastelands*; King
is the victim of a frivolous lawsuit; Tabitha King encounters
an intruder in their house; *Needful Things* is published.

1992   *Sleepwalkers* and *The Lawnmower Man* movies released
(the former based on a screenplay by King); *Gerald's Game*
published; performs in a rock band with fellow authors as the
Rock Bottom Remainders; donates money to build a ballpark
in Bangor.

1993   Film adaptation of *The Dark Half* released; miniseries of *The
Tommyknockers* airs on ABC; *Nightmares & Dreamscapes*
collection and *Dolores Claiborne* published.

1994 *Insomnia* published; miniseries of *The Stand* airs on ABC; film release of *The Shawshank Redemption*.

1995 *Rose Madder* published; films of *Dolores Claiborne* and *The Mangler*; ABC miniseries of *The Langoliers* (from *Four Past Midnight*).

1996 Wins First Prize in O. Henry Awards for his story "The Man in the Black Suit"; *Desperation*, *The Regulators*, and *The Green Mile* published.

1997 Miniseries re-make of *The Shining*; limited edition of *Six Stories*; publishes *The Dark Tower IV: Wizard and Glass*; begins to write "The Pop of King" column for *Entertainment Weekly*, rides a Harley across some of Australia; switches publishers.

1998 Scribner publishes *Bag of Bones*.

1999 *Storm of the Century* miniseries airs; *The Girl Who Loved Tom Gordon* and *Hearts in Atlantis* published; accident and recovery.

2000 Continues to recover from the accident; publishes *On Writing: A Memoir of the Craft*.

2001 Publishes *Dreamcatcher*, which he wrote in longhand, lying down; re-teams with Peter Straub to publish *Black House*, the sequel to *The Talisman*.

2002 Announces he will stop writing after the publication of five more books; publishes *From a Buick 8* and *Everything's Eventual*.

2003 Publishes *The Dark Tower V: The Wolves of the Calla*; awarded National Book Foundation Medal for Distinguished Contribution to American Letters and Lifetime Achievement Award from the Horror Writer's Association.

2004 Completes the "Dark Tower" series with *The Dark Tower VI: Song of Susannah* and *The Dark Tower VII: The Dark Tower*; chronicles the Red Sox championship season with Steward O'Nan in *Faithful*; produces *Kingdom Hospital* miniseries.

2005 Publishes his first crime novel, *The Colorado Kid*.

2006 Publishes *Cell* and *Lisey's Story*.

2007 Publishes *Blaze* (as Richard Bachman).

2008 Publishes his latest novel, *Duma Key*; continues work on his upcoming musical, *The Ghost Brothers of Darkland County*, with John Cougar Mellencamp.

NOTES

Chapter 1

1 All the facts concerning the accident are drawn from the postscript of King's book, *On Writing: A Memoir of the Craft.* New York: Scribner, 2000, pp. 253–260.

2 Ibid., p. 25.

3 Stephen King, *Danse Macabre.* London: Futura, p. 103.

4 Tim Underwood and Chuck Miller, eds., *Bare Bones: Conversations on Terror with Stephen King.* New York: Warner, 1988, p. 3.

5 King, *On Writing,* p. 28.

6 Ibid., p. 29.

7 Ibid., p. 49.

8 George Beahm, *Stephen King: American's Best-Loved Boogeyman.* Kansas City: Andrews McMeel, 1998, p. 8.

9 King, *On Writing,* p. 45.

10 King, *Danse Macabre,* p. 107.

11 Douglas E. Winter. *Stephen King: The Art of Darkness.* (Expanded and Updated Ed.) New York: Plume, 1986, p. 17.

12 Ibid, p. 18.

13 Ibid. p. 19.

14 Ibid. p. 20.

Chapter 2

1 Winter, *Stephen King: The Art of Darkness,* p. 20.

2 Ibid.

3 Ibid., p. 24.

4 King, *On Writing,* p. 62.

5 Ibid., p. 67.

6 Underwood and Miller, eds., *Bare Bones,* p. 32.

7 Tim Underwood and Chuck Miller, eds., *Feast of Fear: Conversations with Stephen King.* New York: Warner, 1989, p. 7.

Chapter 3

1 Underwood and Miller, eds., *Bare Bones,* p. 33.

2 Winter, *Stephen King: The Art of Darkness,* p. 15.

3 King, *On Writing,* p. 92.

4 E.G. Chelsea Quinn Yarbro, "Cinderella's Revenge: Twists on Fairy Tale and Mythic Themes in the Work of Stephen King," in *Fear Itself: The Horror Fiction of Stephen King* by Tim Underwood and Chuck Miller. New York: Plume, 1982.

5 King, *Danse Macabre,* pp. 198–199.

6 Stephen King, Afterword to *Different Seasons.* New York: New American Library, 1982, p. 504.

7 Beahm, *Stephen King: America's Best-Loved Boogeyman,* p. 34.

8 Underwood and Miller, eds., *Fear Itself,* p. 10.

Chapter 4

1 Underwood and Millers, eds., *Fear Itself*, p. 40.

2 Beahm, *Stephen King: America's Best-Loved Boogeyman*, p. 40.

3 Winter, *Stephen King: The Art of Darkness*, p. 76.

4 Ibid., p. 76.

5 Beahm, *Stephen King: America's Best-Loved Boogeyman*, p. 45.

6 Ibid., p. 44.

7 Winter, *Stephen King: The Art of Darkness*, p. 76.

Chapter 5

1 King, Afterword to *Different Seasons*, p. 501.

2 Winter, *Stephen King: The Art of Darkness*, p. 175.

3 Stephen King, "Why I Was Bachman," introduction to *The Bachman Books*. New York: Signet, 1986, p. xi.

4 Winter, *Stephen King: The Art of Darkness*, p. 176.

5 Beahm, *Stephen King: America's Best-Loved Boogeyman*, p. 99.

6 King, "Why I Was Bachman," p. xi.

7 The phrase, popularized by Edgar Allan Poe in a short story of the same name, can be loosely defined as the strong desire to do something, "merely because we feel we should *not*."

8 Winter, *Stephen King: The Art of Darkness*, p. 131.

9 Beahm, *Stephen King: America's Best-Loved Boogeyman*, p. 57.

10 Underwood and Miller, eds., *Bare Bones*, p. 29.

11 Beahm, *Stephen King: America's Best-Loved Boogeyman*, p. 62.

Chapter 6

1 Winter, *Stephen King: The Art of Darkness*, p. 164.

2 Ibid., p. 172.

3 King, "Why I Was Bachman," p. xii.

4 Beahm, *Stephen King: America's Best-Loved Boogeyman*, p. 72.

5 Winter, *Stephen King: The Art of Darkness*, pp. 131–132.

6 Beahm, *Stephen King: America's Best-Loved Boogeyman*, p. 75.

7 Ibid., p. 77.

Chapter 7

1 George Beahm, *The Stephen King Story: A Literary Profile.* Kansas City: Andrews & McMeel, 1991, p. 138.

2 King, On Writing, p. 97.

3 Ibid., p. 98.

4 Ibid., p. 97.

5 Ibid., p. 99.

Chapter 8

1 Beahm, *The Stephen King Story*, pp. 163–164.

Chapter 9

1 Stephen King, "The Pop of King," EW.com. www.ew.com/ew/article/0,,20056512,00.html.

2 Stephen King, "Fresh Air with Terry Gross," radio interview, June 22, 2001.

3 Kim Murphy, "House Master," *Los Angeles Times*. (January 27, 2002): p 96.

Chapter 10

1 Stephen King, afterword to *The Dark Tower: The Gunslinger*. New York: Plume, p. 222.

2 Ibid., p. 219.

3 Harold Bloom, "Dumbing Down American Readers," Boston.com. www.boston.com/news/globe/editorial_opinion/oped/articles/2003/09/24/dumbing_down_american_readers/

4 Stephen King. National Book Award acceptance speech, 2003. National Book Foundation. www.nationalbook.org/nbaacceptspeech_sking.html.

5 King, "The Pop of King," EW.com www.ew.com/ew/article/0,,472420,00.html.

WORKS BY
STEPHEN KING

1974 *Carrie*

1975 *'Salem's Lot*

1977 *The Shining*; *Rage* (as Richard Bachman)

1978 *The Stand*; *Night Shift*

1979 *The Dead Zone*; *The Long Walk* (as Richard Bachman)

1980 *Danse Macabre*; *Firestarter*

1981 *Cujo*; *Roadwork* (as Richard Bachman)

1982 *The Dark Tower: The Gunslinger*; *Different Seasons*; *Roadwork* (as Richard Bachman)

1983 *Christine*; *Pet Sematary*; *Cycle of the Werewolf*

1984 *The Talisman*; *Thinner* (as Richard Bachman)

1985 *Skeleton Crew*

1986 *IT*; *The Eyes of the Dragon*

1987 *Misery*; *The Tommyknockers*; *The Dark Tower II: The Drawing of the Three*

1988 *Nightmares in the Sky: Gargoyles and Grotesques* (with f-stop Fitzgerald)

1989 *The Dark Half*

1990 *Four Past Midnight*; *The Stand: The Complete and Uncut Edition*

1991 *The Dark Tower III: The Wastelands*; *Needful Things*

1992 *Dolores Claiborne*; *Gerald's Game*

1993 *Nightmares and Dreamscapes*; *Gray Matter and Other Stories*

1994 *Insomnia*

1995 *Rose Madder*

1996 *Desperation*; *The Green Mile*; *The Regulators* (as Richard Bachman)

1997 *Six Stories*; *The Dark Tower IV: Wizard and Glass*

1998 *Bag of Bones*

1999 *Hearts in Atlantis*; *The Girl Who Loved Tom Gordon*

2000 *On Writing: A Memoir of the Craft*

2001 *Dreamcatcher*

2002 *From a Buick 8*; *Everything's Eventual: 14 Dark Tales*; *The Man in the Black Suit: 4 Dark Tales*

2003 *The Dark Tower V: The Wolves of the Calla*

2004 *Faithful* (with Stewart O'Nan); *The Dark Tower VI: Song of Susannah*; *The Dark Tower VII: The Dark Tower*

2005 *The Colorado Kid*

2006 *Cell*; *Lisey's Story*; *The Secretary of Dreams*

2007 *Blaze* (as Richard Bachman)

2008 *Duma Key*

POPULAR BOOKS

THE SHINING

A psychic boy, his mother, and his troubled father try to survive the winter as caretakers of a haunted hotel in Colorado.

THE STAND

When a superflu kills off the majority of humanity, the survivors band together into two camps and wage a final confrontation between good and evil.

PET SEMATARY

A father gets more than he bargained for when he buries his dead child in an animal cemetery with the power of resurrection.

IT

Six children wound an ancient evil in the sewers of their town; 25 years later they must face it again as adults.

THE GREEN MILE

A prison guard is forced to accept the existence of the supernatural when he is healed by a huge but simple-minded Death Row inmate.

POPULAR CHARACTERS

CARRIE WHITE

A homely teenage girl who discovers telekinetic powers and wreaks revenge on her high school tormentors.

DANNY TORRANCE

The psychic boy in *The Shining* who battles a whole host of ghosts as his father is driven insane. Memorably portrayed by Danny Lloyd in Stanley Kubrick's 1980 film adaptation.

ROLAND OF GILEAD

The Gunslinger in King's epic Dark Tower series. Named after the title character in Robert Browning's classic poem "Childe Roland to the Dark Tower Came."

ANNIE WILKES

The crazy fan in *Misery* who kidnaps writer Paul Sheldon and forces him to bring back her favorite romance novel character. Kathy Bates won an Oscar for her portrayal of Annie Wilkes in the 1990 film version.

IT

The ancient evil from the book of the same name. Appears in many forms, including as a huge spider and a clown called Pennywise.

MAJOR AWARDS

1982 King wins the World Fantasy Award for Best Short Fiction ("Do the Dead Sing") and the Hugo Award (*Danse Macabre*).

1995 King wins the World Fantasy Award for Best Short Fiction ("The Man in the Black Suit").

1996 King receives the O. Henry Award ("The Man in the Black Suit").

2003 King honored with a Lifetime Achievement Award from the Horror Writer's Association and National Book Foundation Medal for Distinguished Contribution to American Letters.

2004 King receives the World Fantasy Award for Lifetime Achievement.

2005 King wins the Quill Award for Sports Writing (*Faithful*).

* Plus numerous Bram Stoker, Horror Guild, and Locus Awards for various novels and story collections (various years)

BIBLIOGRAPHY

Beahm, George. *Stephen King: America's Best-Loved Boogeyman*. Kansas City: Andrews and McMeel, 1998.

———. *Stephen King from A to Z: An Encyclopedia of His Life and Work*. Kansas City: Andrews and McMeel, 1998.

———. *The Stephen King Companion*. Kansas City: Andrews and McMeel, 1989.

———. *The Stephen King Story*. Kansas City: Andrews and McMeel, 1991.

Collings, Michael. *Stephen King as Richard Bachman*. Mercer Island, Wash.: Starmont House, 1985.

King, Stephen. *Danse Macabre*. London: Futura, 1982.

———. *On Writing: A Memoir of the Craft*. New York: Scribner, 2000.

———. "Why I Was Bachman." Introduction to *The Bachman Books*. New York: Signet, 1986.

Underwood, Tim, and Chuck Miller, eds. *Bare Bones: Conversations on Terror with Stephen King*. New York: Warner, 1988.

———. *Fear Itself: The Horror Fiction of Stephen King*. New York: Plume, 1982.

———. *Feast of Fear: Conversations with Stephen King*. New York: Warner, 1989.

Winter, Douglas E. *Stephen King: The Art of Darkness*. Rev. and exp. ed. New York: Plume, 1986.

FURTHER READING

Blue, Tyson. *The Unseen King*. Mercer Island, Wash.: Starmont House, 1989.

Collings, Michael R. *The Films of Stephen King*. Mercer Island, Wash.: Starmont House, 1986.

———. *The Stephen King Concordance*. Mercer Island, Wash.: Starmont House, 1985.

———. *The Stephen King Phenomenon*. Mercer Island, Wash.: Starmont House, 1986.

Russell, Sharon A. *Stephen King: A Critical Companion*. Westport, Conn.: Greenwood Press, 1996.

———. *Revisiting Stephen King: A Critical Companion*. Westport, Conn.: Greenwood Press, 2002.

Spignesi, Stephen J. *The Essential Stephen King: A Ranking of the Greatest Novels, Short Stories, Movies, and Other Creations of the World's Most Popular Writer*. Franklin Lakes, N.J.: New Page Books, 2003.

Strengell, Heidi. *Dissecting Stephen King: From the Gothic to Literary Naturalism*. Madison, Wisc.: University of Wisconsin Press, 2005.

Terrell, Carol F. *Stephen King: Man and Artist*. Orono, Maine: Northern Lights, 1991.

Wiater, Stanley, Christopher Golden, and Hank Wagner. *The Complete Stephen King Universe: A Guide to the Worlds of Stephen King*. New York: St. Martin's Press, 2006.

Web Sites

Horror King
http://www.horrorking.com

Stephen King.net
http://stephen-king.net

Stephen King—Official Website
http://www.stephenking.com

INDEX

ABOUT THE CONTRIBUTOR

MICHAEL GRAY BAUGHAN is a freelance writer and researcher. When he isn't working, he can usually be found running around after his twin daughters, Callie and Ella, or trailing his archaeologist wife, Elizabeth, into parts unknown. In addition to the present volume, he has written biographies of Shel Silverstein and Charles Bukowski, as well as research guides to the works of E.E. Cummings, Rudyard Kipling, and John Ashbery.

PICTURE CREDITS

page:

10:   Mario Magnani/Getty

22:   Shel Hershorn / Time Magazine, Copyright Time Inc./Time Life Pictures/Getty Images

29:   Courtesy of Hampden Academy

32:   UA/Photofest

37:   Columbia Pictures/Photofest

42:   Jeffrey Vock/Getty Images

49:   Warner Bros./Photofest

52:   Ted Thai/Time Life Pictures/Getty Images

64:   Time & Life Pictures/Getty Images

76:   AP Images

81:   Robin Platzer/Film Magic/Getty Images

86:   Kevin Higley/AP Images

93:   Photofest, Inc.

96:   © John-Marshall Mantel/CORBIS

106:   Jennifer Graylock/AP Images

114:   Ted Thai/Time & Life Pictures/Getty Images

LAKE OSWEGO JR. HIGH SCHOOL
2500 SW COUNTRY CLUB RD
LAKE OSWEGO, OR 97034
503-534-2335